DreamW

DRAGONS
RIDERS OF BERK

VOLUME ONE

DRAGON DOWN

SCRIPT
SIMON FURMAN

PENCILS
IWAN NAZIF

INKS
IWAN NAZIF
WITH **BAMBOS GEORGIOU** (35, 40-48)

COLORING
NESTOR PEREYRA
& DIGIKORE

LETTERING
DAVID MANLEY-LEACH

TITAN
COMICS

DreamWorks Dragons: Riders of Berk

TITAN EDITORIAL

Senior Editor
MARTIN EDEN

Production Manager
OBI ONOURA

Production Supervisors
PETER JAMES, JACKIE FLOOK

Studio Manager
SELINA JUNEJA

Circulation Manager
STEVE TOTHILL

Marketing Manager
RICKY CLAYDON

Publishing Manager
DARRYL TOTHILL

Publishing Director
CHRIS TEATHER

Operations Director
LEIGH BAULCH

Executive Director
VIVIAN CHEUNG

Publisher
NICK LANDAU

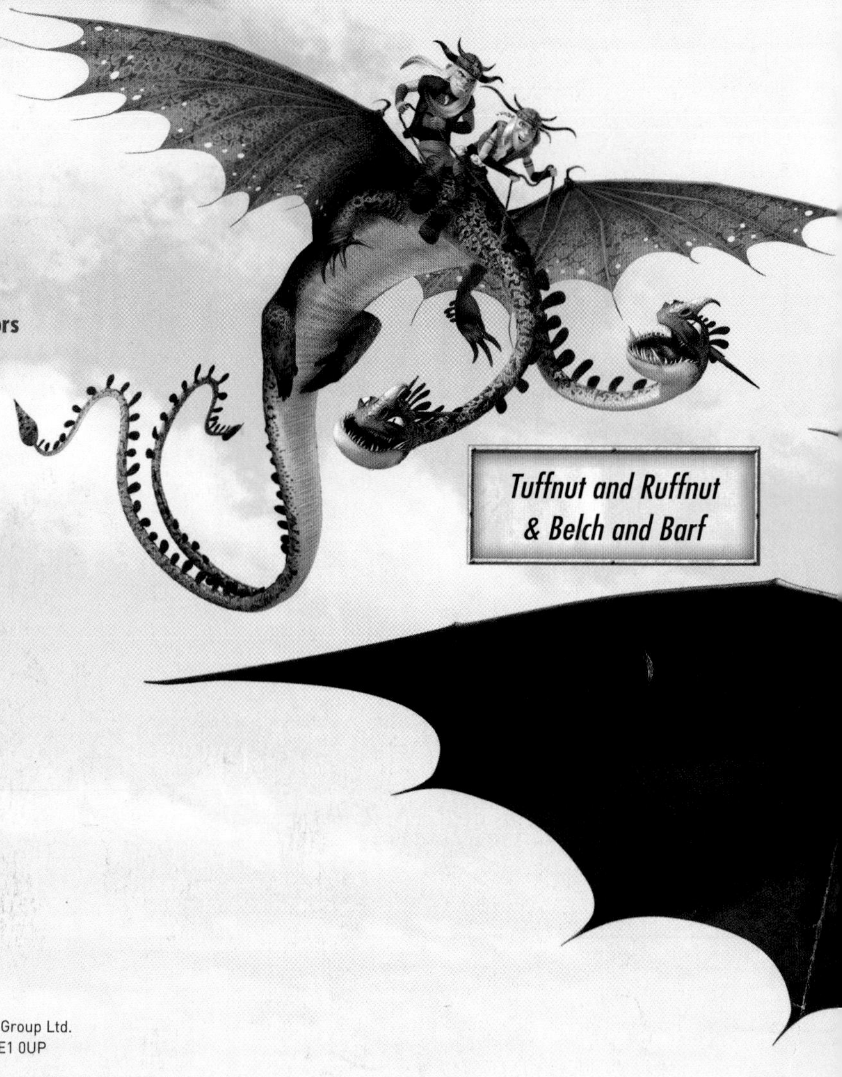
Tuffnut and Ruffnut
& Belch and Barf

ISBN: 9781782760764
Published by Titan Comics,
a division of Titan Publishing Group Ltd.
144 Southwark St. London, SE1 0UP

10 9 8 7 6 5 4 3 2 1
First printed in the United States of America in March 2014.
A CIP catalogue record for this title is available from the British Library.
Titan Comics. TC0158

Special thanks to Corinne Combs, Alyssa Mauney and all at DreamWorks. Also to Andre Siregar at Glass House Graphics.

DREAMWORKS
DRAGONS
RIDERS OF BERK

VOLUME ONE

DRAGON DOWN

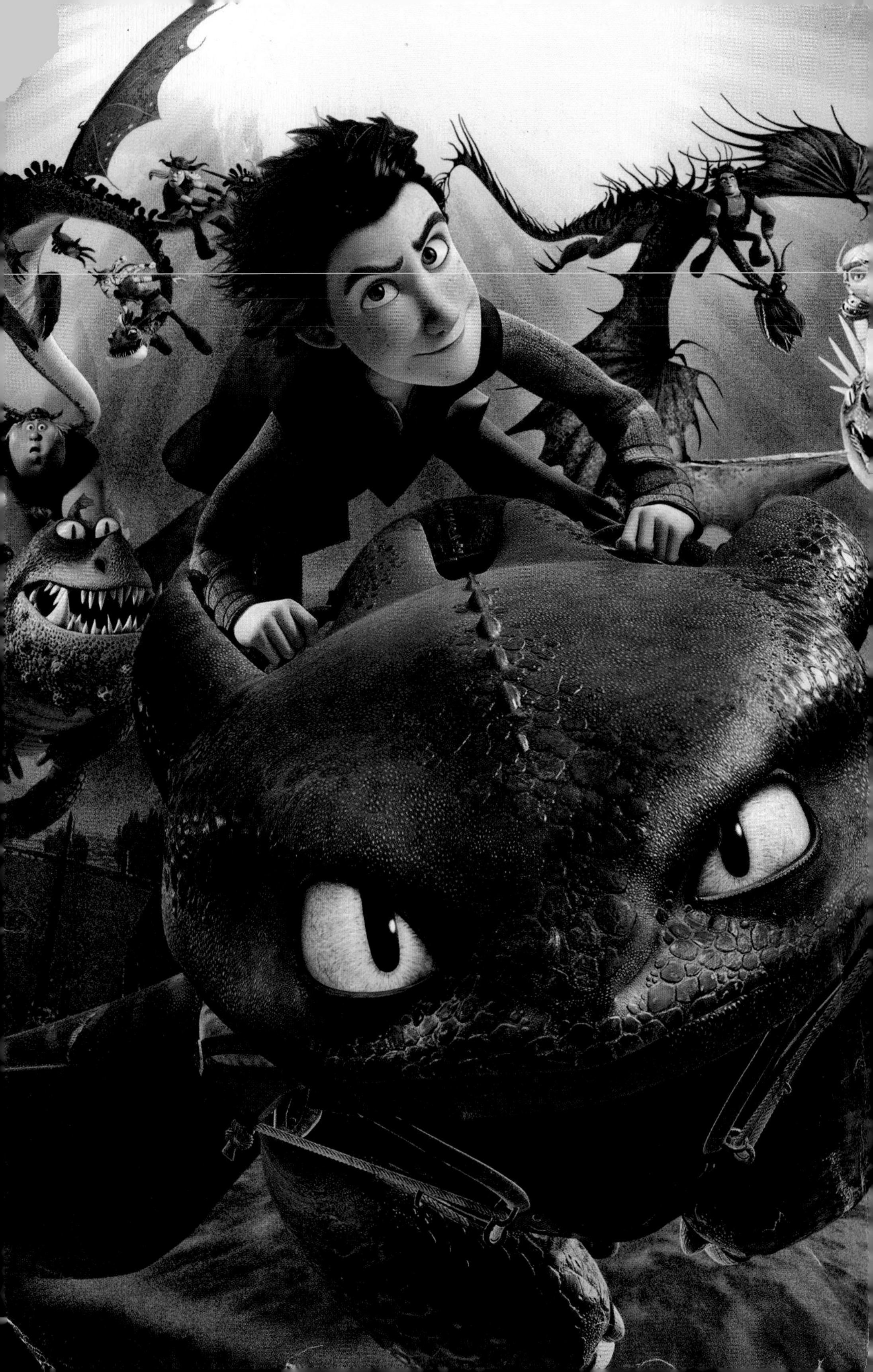

Welcome to Berk, the home of Hiccup and his dragon Toothless, plus Hiccup's friends who train at the Dragon Training Academy! And let's not forget all the Vikings and dragons…

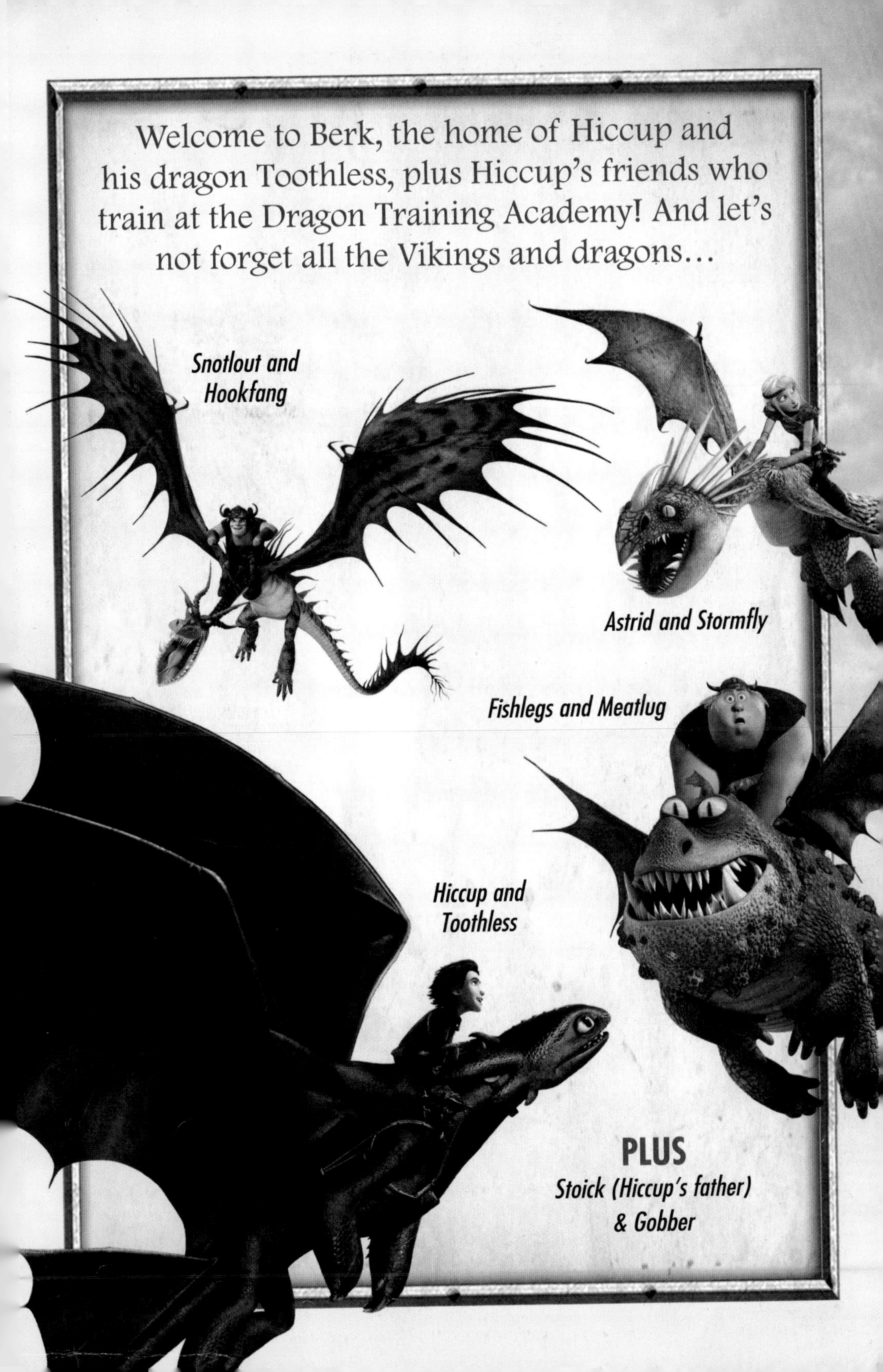
Snotlout and Hookfang
Astrid and Stormfly
Fishlegs and Meatlug
Hiccup and Toothless
PLUS
Stoick (Hiccup's father) & Gobber

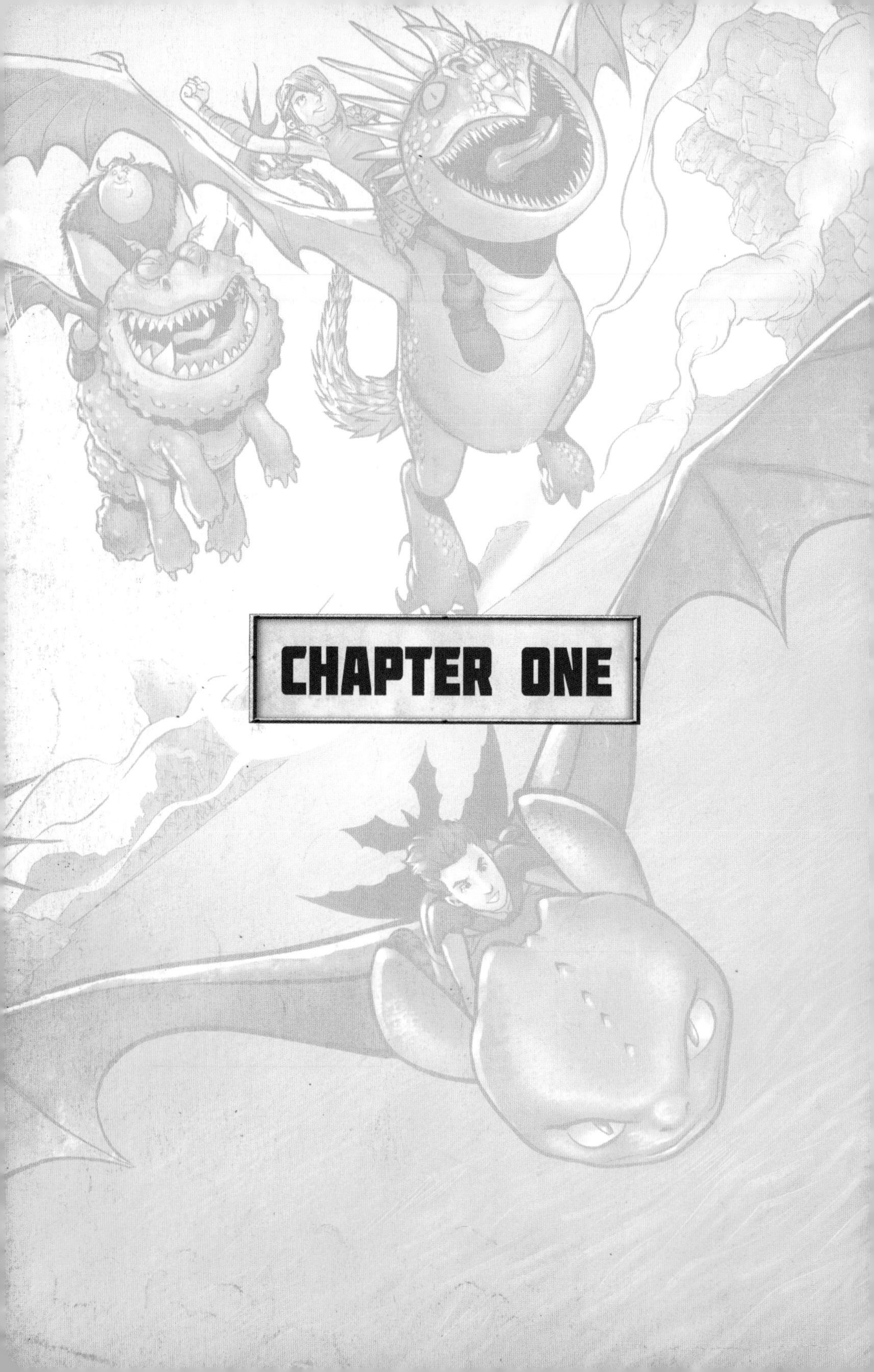

CHAPTER ONE

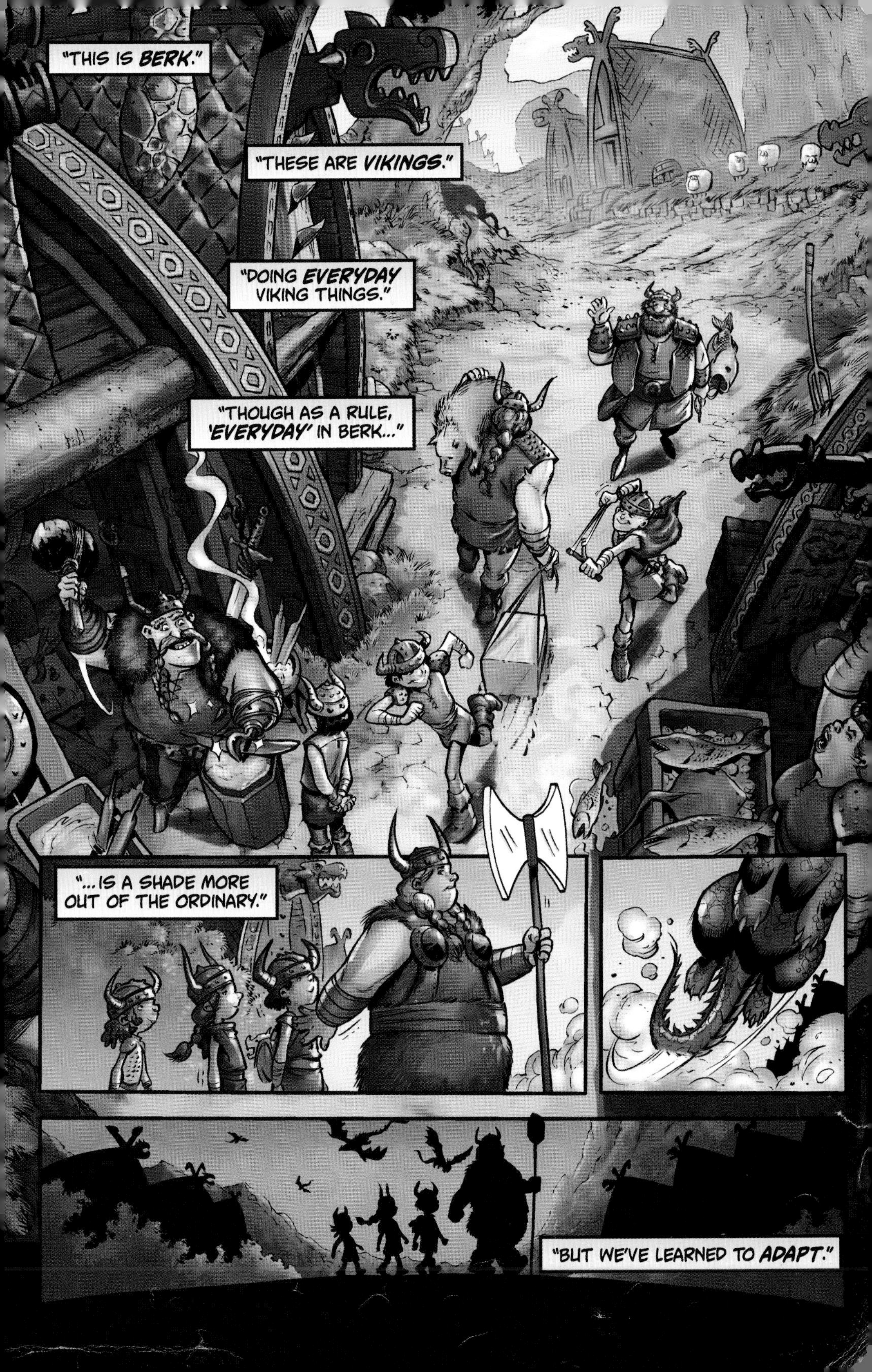
"THIS IS BERK."
"THESE ARE VIKINGS."
"DOING EVERYDAY VIKING THINGS."
"THOUGH AS A RULE, 'EVERYDAY' IN BERK..."
"...IS A SHADE MORE OUT OF THE ORDINARY."
"BUT WE'VE LEARNED TO ADAPT."

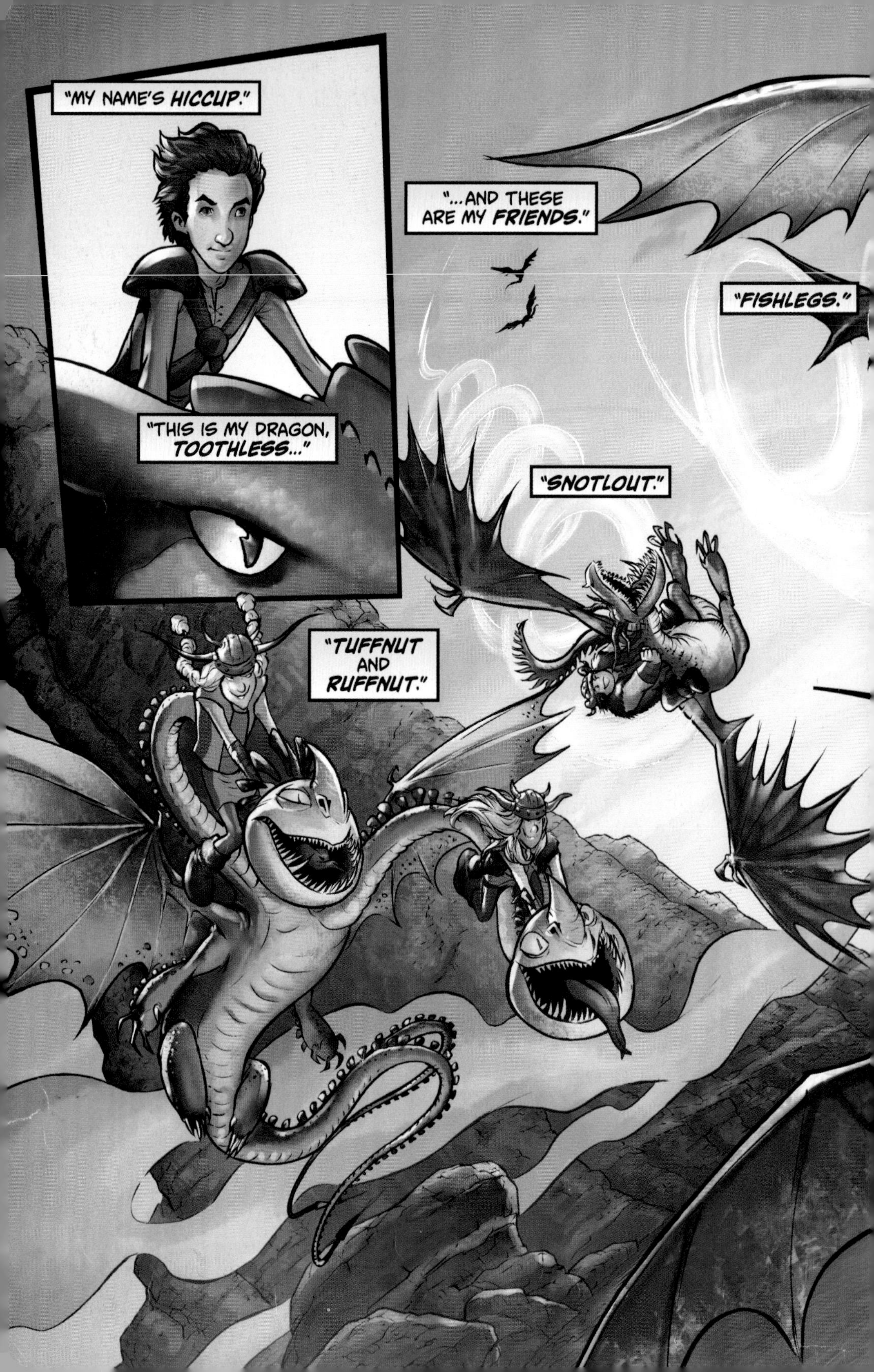
"MY NAME'S HICCUP."
"THIS IS MY DRAGON, TOOTHLESS..."
"...AND THESE ARE MY FRIENDS."
"FISHLEGS."
"SNOTLOUT."
"TUFFNUT AND RUFFNUT."

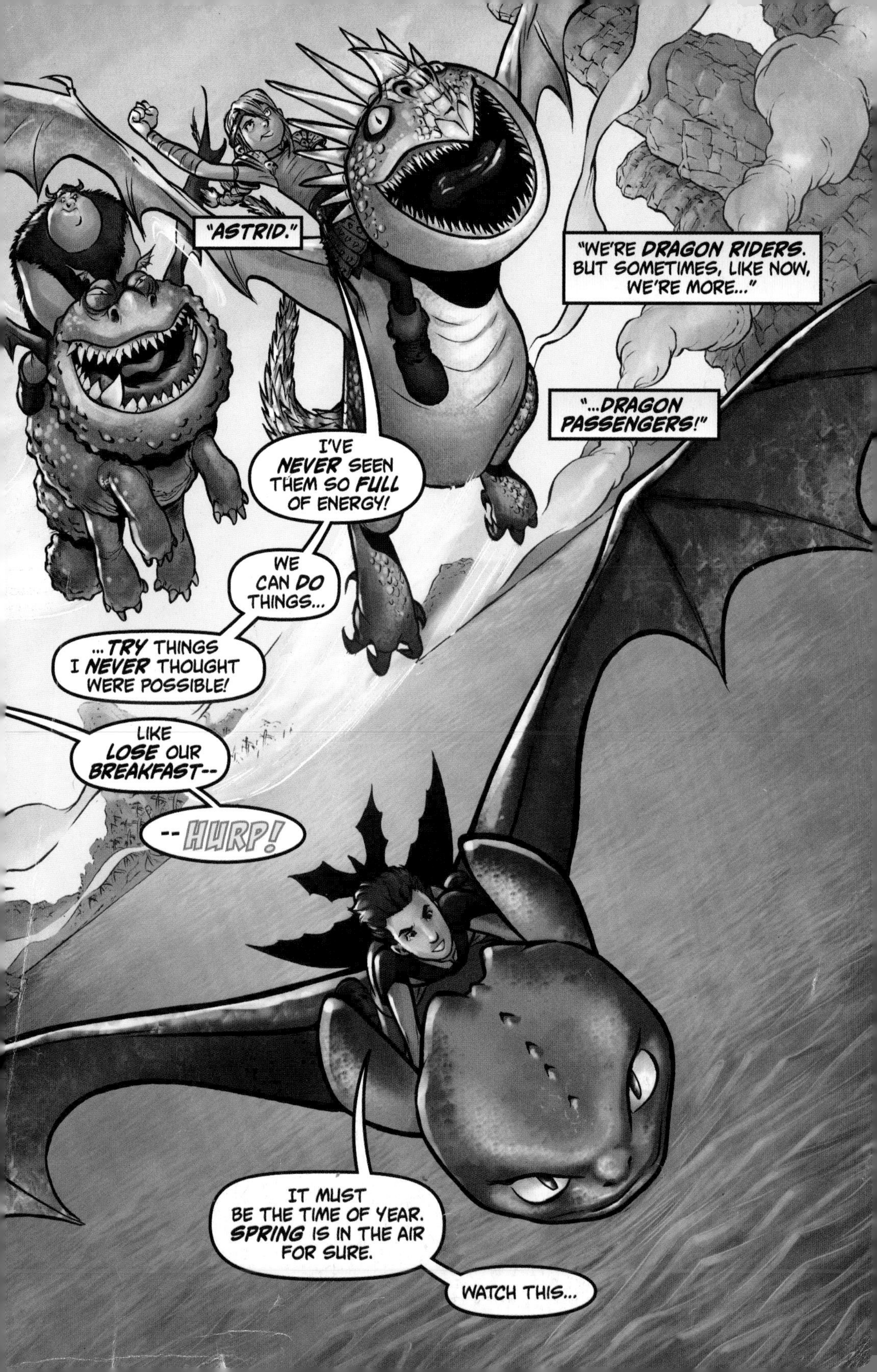
"ASTRID."
"WE'RE DRAGON RIDERS. BUT SOMETIMES, LIKE NOW, WE'RE MORE..."
"...DRAGON PASSENGERS!"
I'VE NEVER SEEN THEM SO FULL OF ENERGY!
WE CAN DO THINGS...
...TRY THINGS I NEVER THOUGHT WERE POSSIBLE!
LIKE LOSE OUR BREAKFAST--
--HURP!
IT MUST BE THE TIME OF YEAR. SPRING IS IN THE AIR FOR SURE.
WATCH THIS...

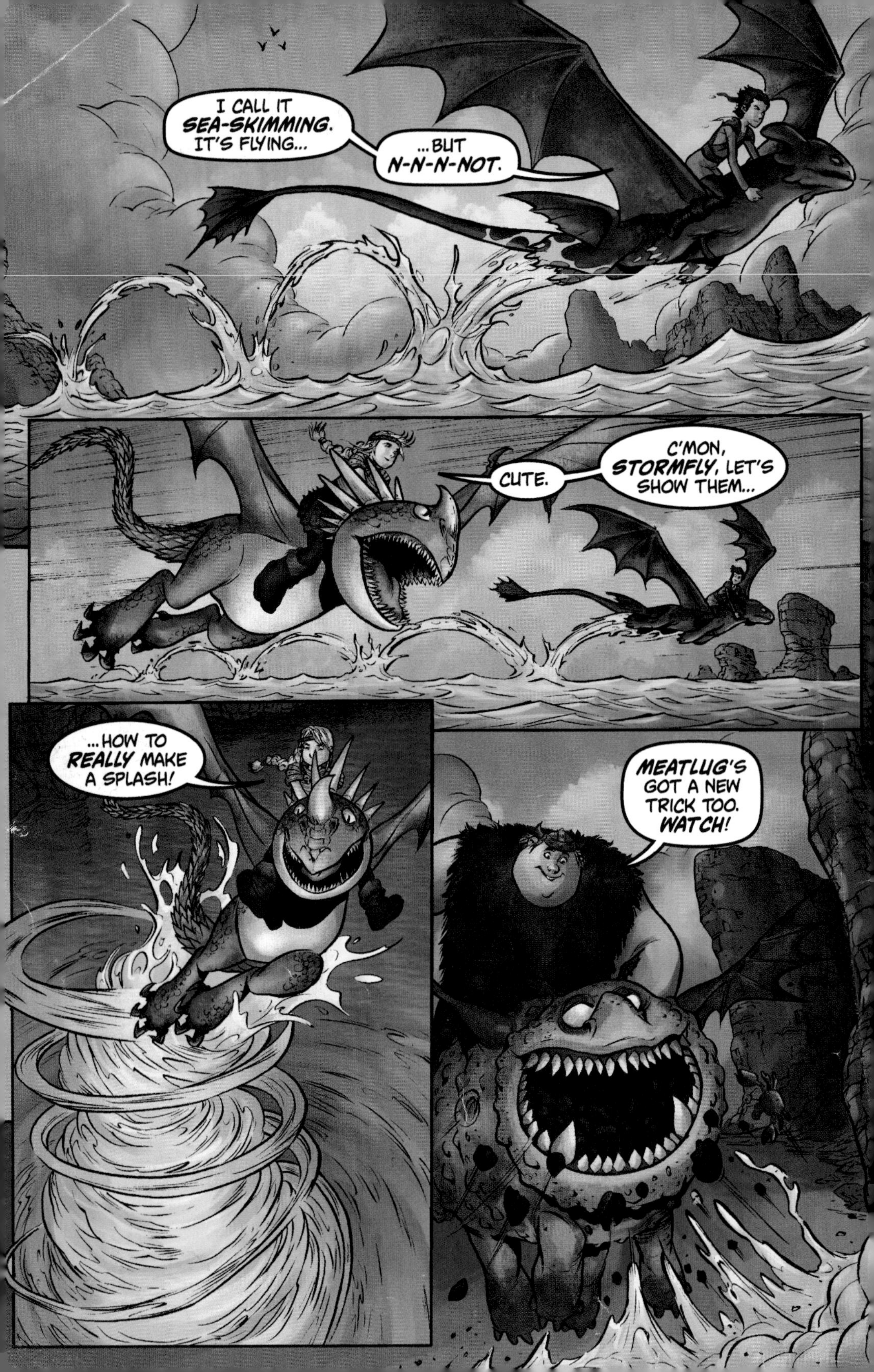
I CALL IT SEA-SKIMMING. IT'S FLYING...
...BUT N-N-N-NOT.
CUTE.
C'MON, STORMFLY, LET'S SHOW THEM...
...HOW TO REALLY MAKE A SPLASH!
MEATLUG'S GOT A NEW TRICK TOO. WATCH!

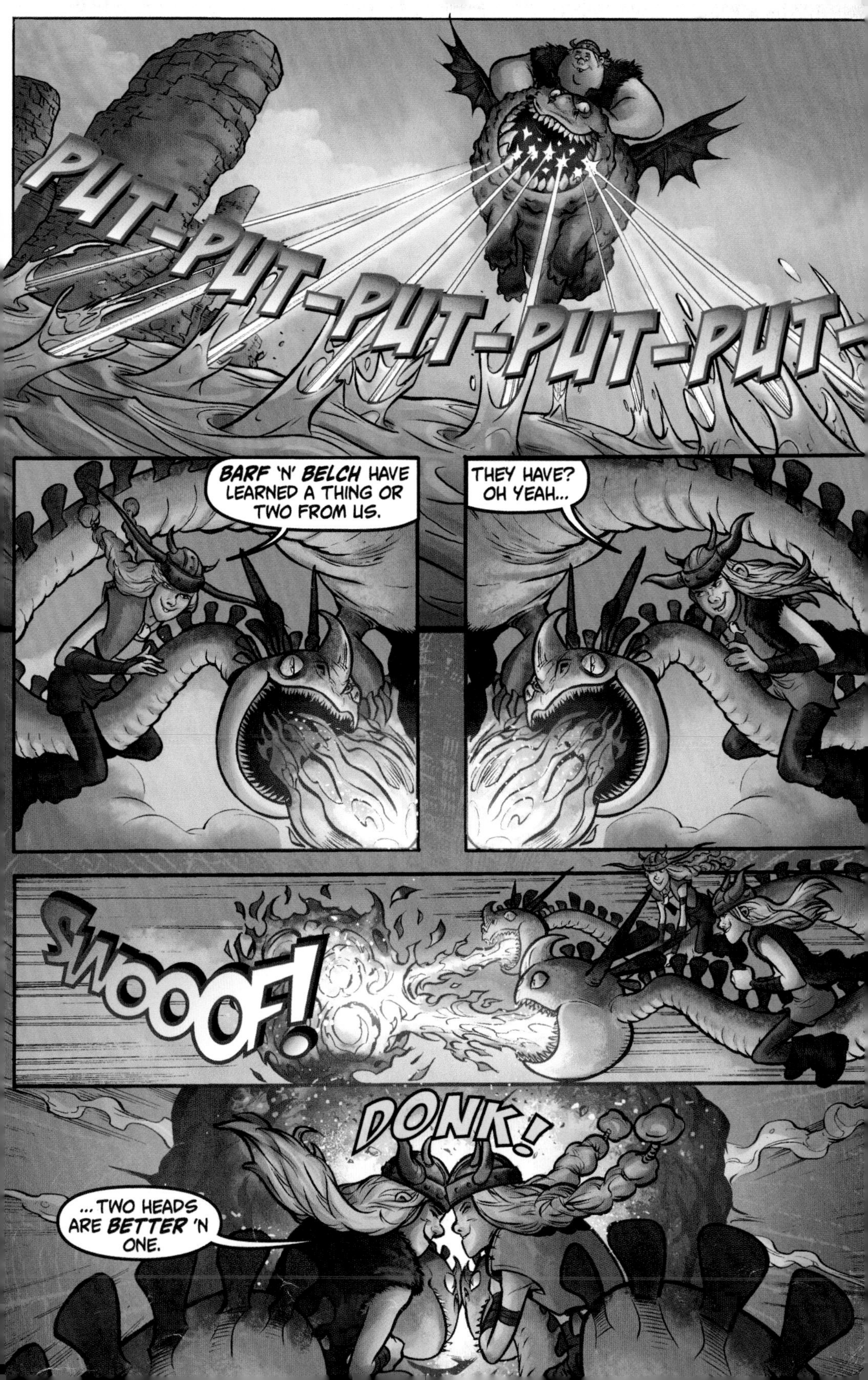
PUT-PUT-PUT-PUT-PUT-
BARF 'N' BELCH HAVE LEARNED A THING OR TWO FROM US.
THEY HAVE? OH YEAH...
SWOOOF!
DONK!
...TWO HEADS ARE BETTER 'N ONE.

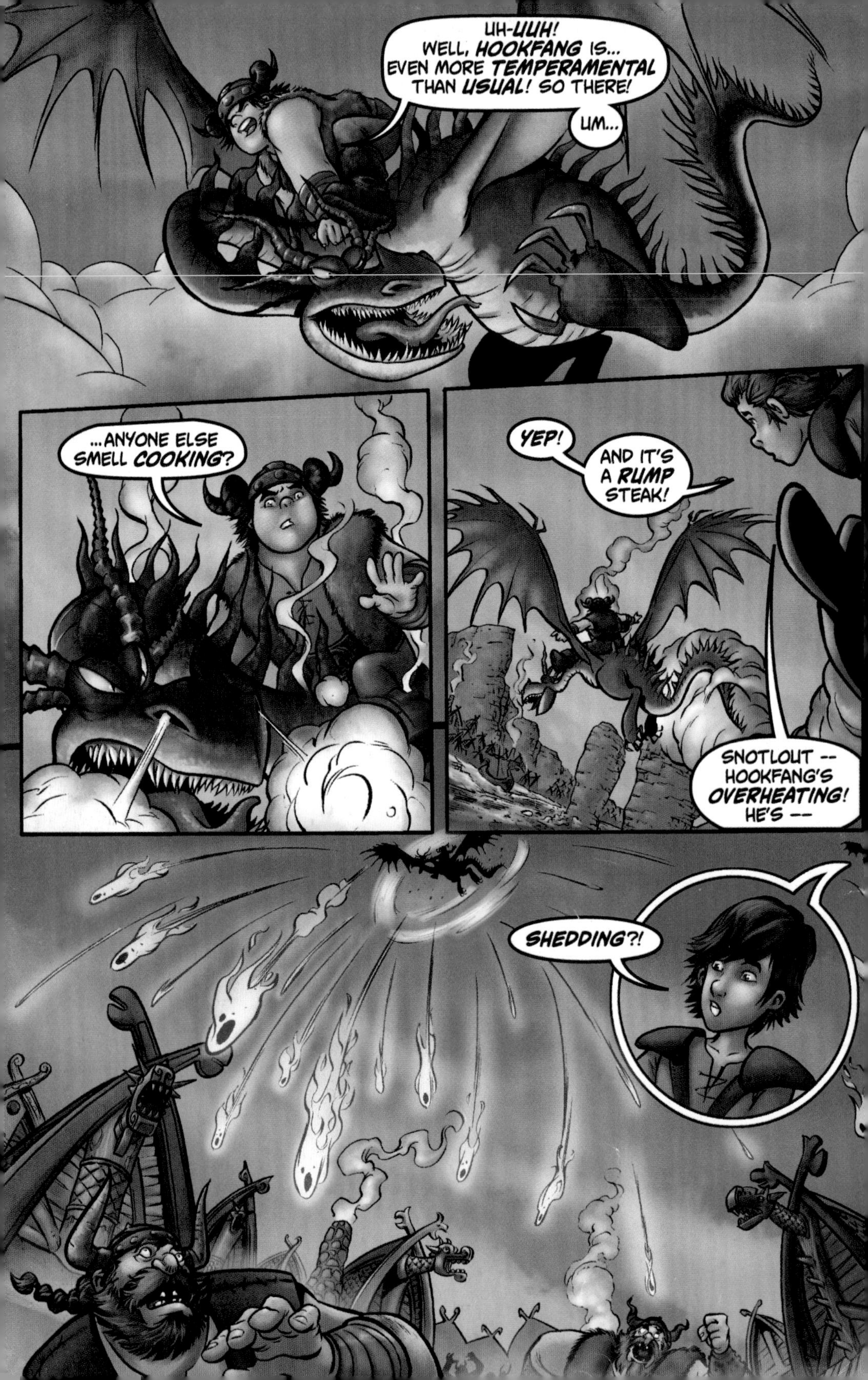
UH-*UUH*! WELL, *HOOKFANG* IS... EVEN MORE *TEMPERAMENTAL* THAN *USUAL*! SO THERE!
UM...
...ANYONE ELSE SMELL *COOKING*?
YEP!
AND IT'S A *RUMP* STEAK!
SNOTLOUT -- HOOKFANG'S *OVERHEATING*! HE'S --
SHEDDING?!

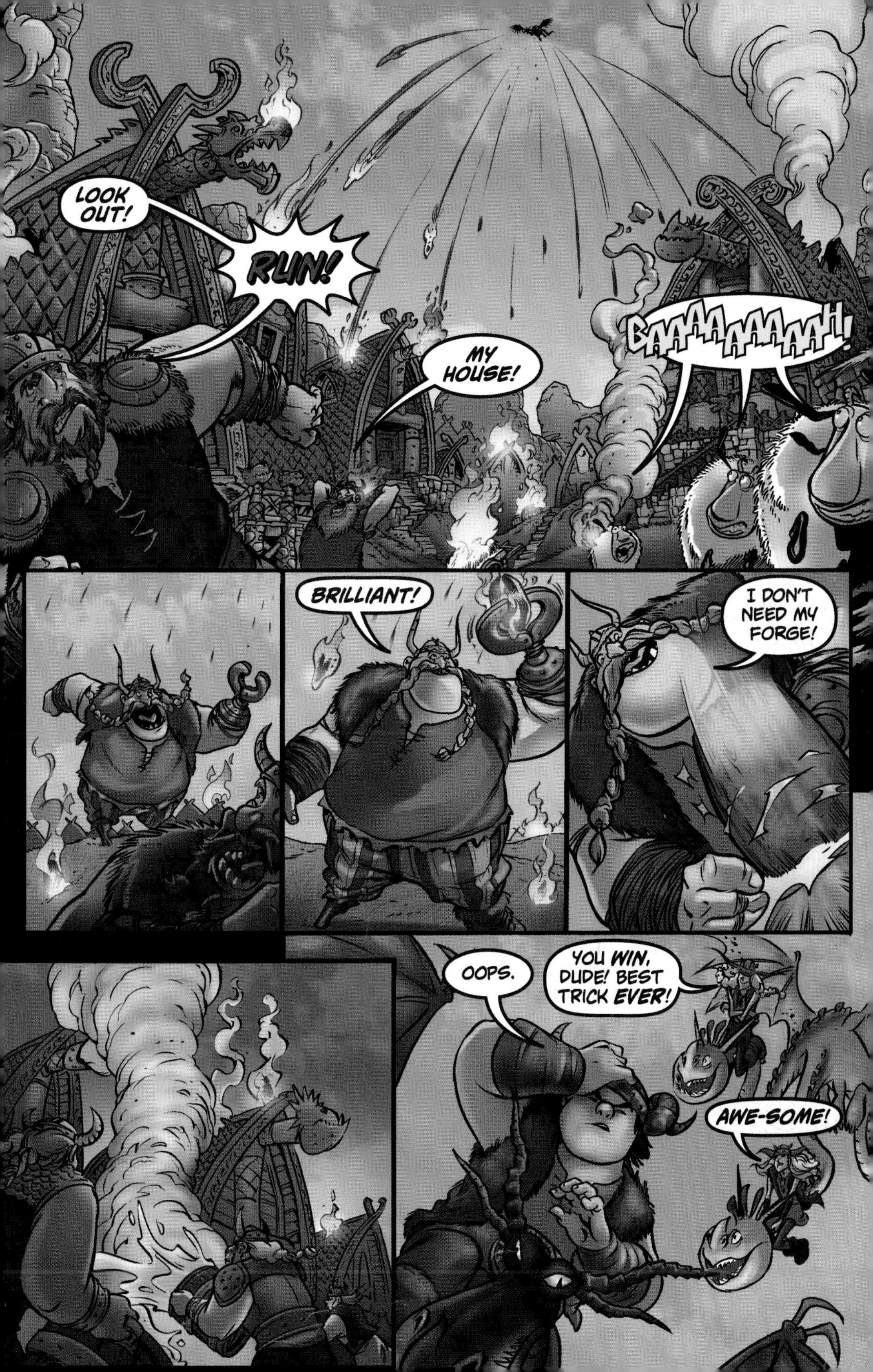
LOOK OUT!
RUN!
MY HOUSE!
BAAAAAAAAAH!
BRILLIANT!
I DON'T NEED MY FORGE!
OOPS.
YOU WIN, DUDE! BEST TRICK EVER!
AWE-SOME!

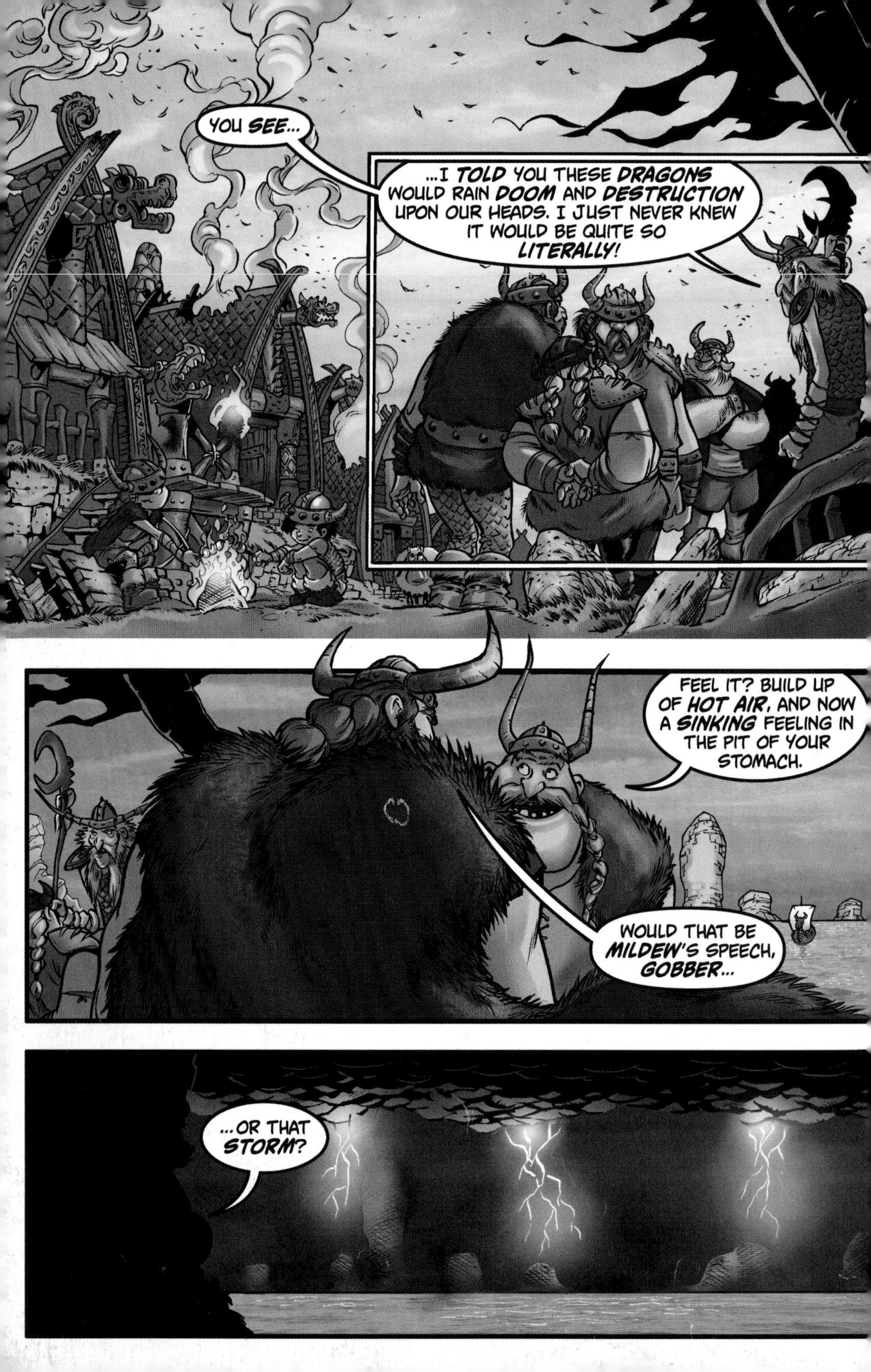
YOU SEE...
...I TOLD YOU THESE DRAGONS WOULD RAIN DOOM AND DESTRUCTION UPON OUR HEADS. I JUST NEVER KNEW IT WOULD BE QUITE SO LITERALLY!
FEEL IT? BUILD UP OF HOT AIR, AND NOW A SINKING FEELING IN THE PIT OF YOUR STOMACH.
WOULD THAT BE MILDEW'S SPEECH, GOBBER...
...OR THAT STORM?

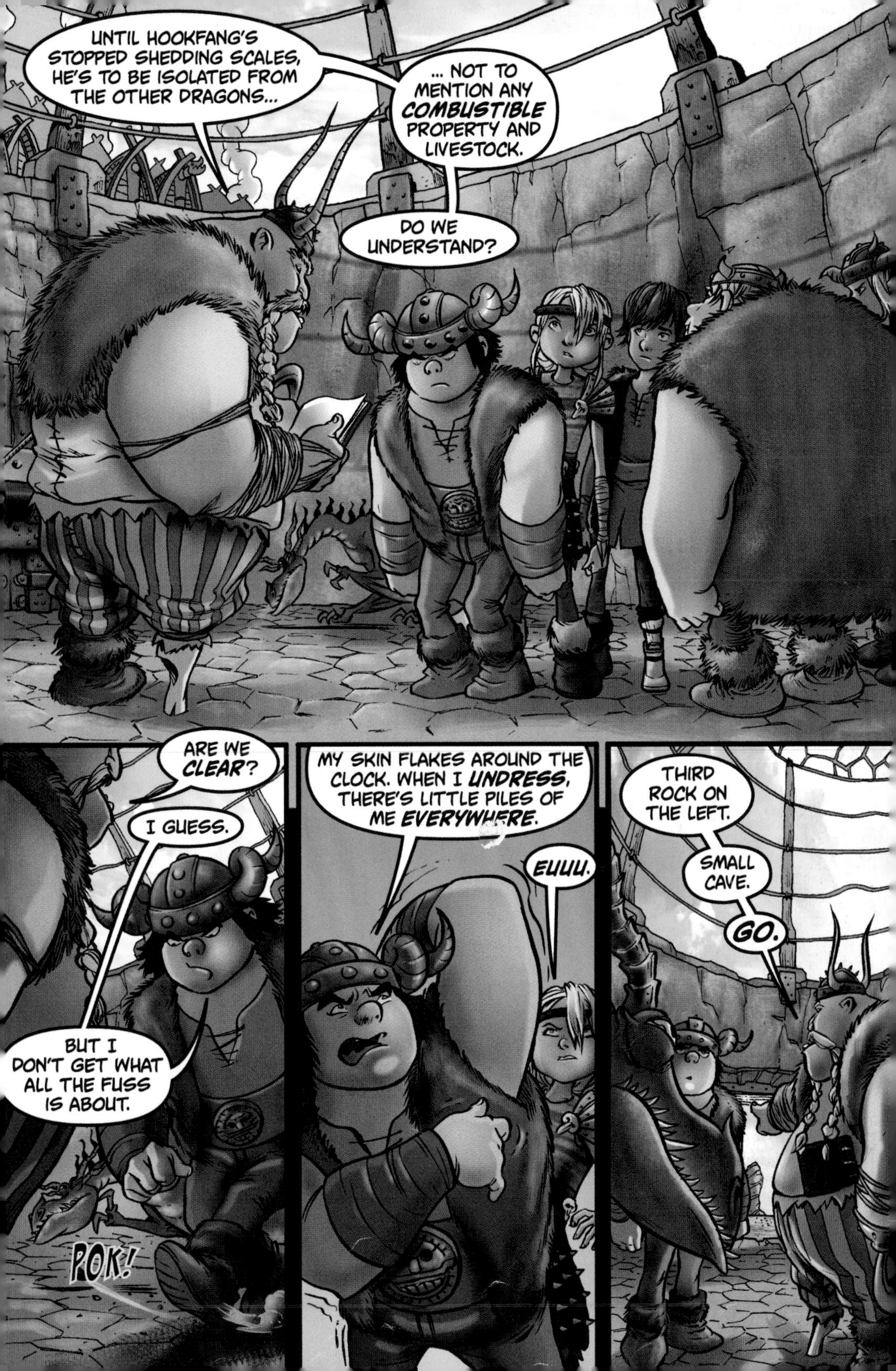
UNTIL HOOKFANG'S STOPPED SHEDDING SCALES, HE'S TO BE ISOLATED FROM THE OTHER DRAGONS...
... NOT TO MENTION ANY COMBUSTIBLE PROPERTY AND LIVESTOCK.
DO WE UNDERSTAND?
ARE WE CLEAR?
I GUESS.
BUT I DON'T GET WHAT ALL THE FUSS IS ABOUT.
POK!
MY SKIN FLAKES AROUND THE CLOCK. WHEN I UNDRESS, THERE'S LITTLE PILES OF ME EVERYWHERE.
EUUU.
THIRD ROCK ON THE LEFT.
SMALL CAVE.
GO.

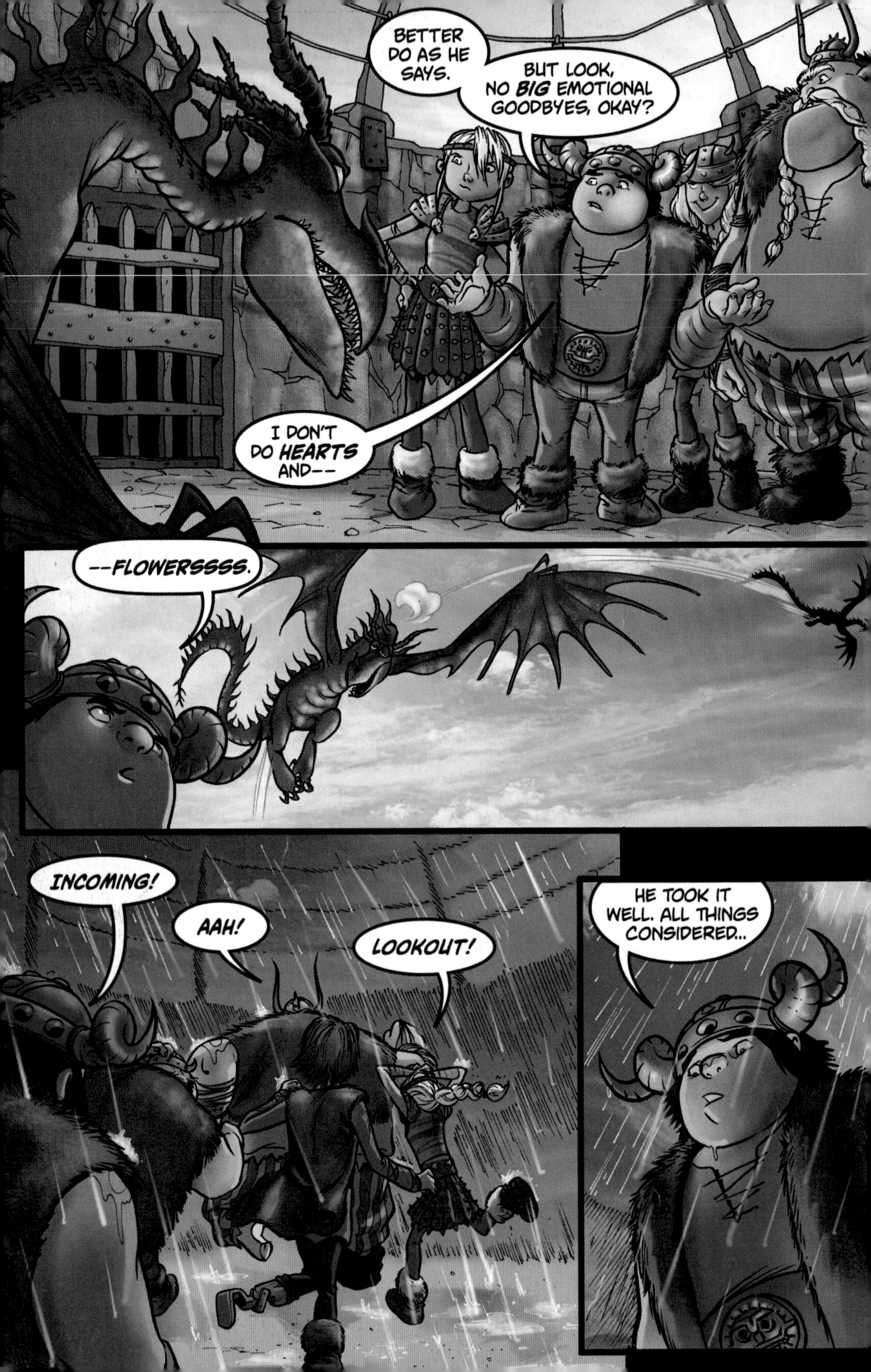
BETTER DO AS HE SAYS.
BUT LOOK, NO BIG EMOTIONAL GOODBYES, OKAY?
I DON'T DO HEARTS AND--
--FLOWERSSSS.
INCOMING!
AAH!
LOOKOUT!
HE TOOK IT WELL. ALL THINGS CONSIDERED...

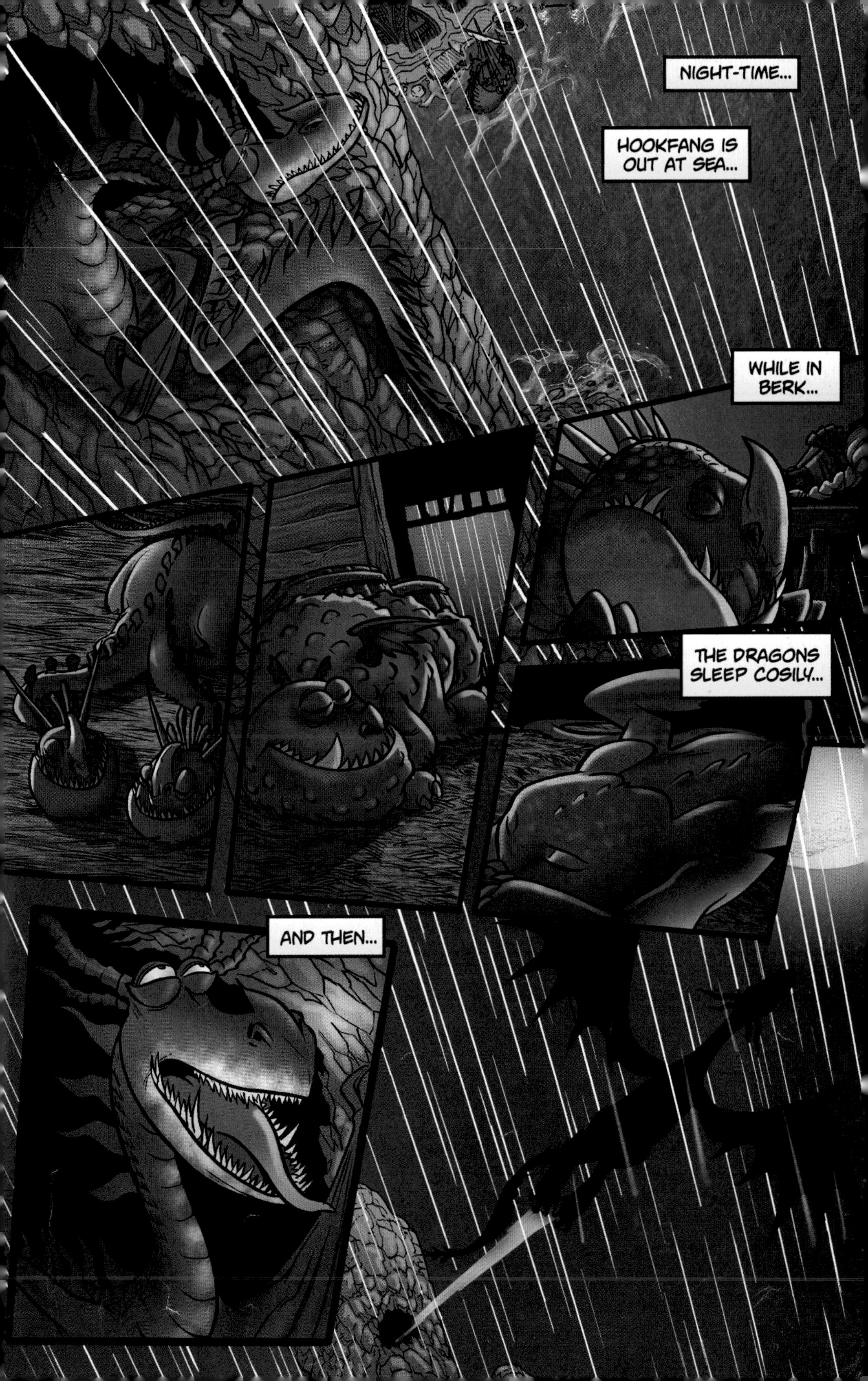
NIGHT-TIME...
HOOKFANG IS OUT AT SEA...
WHILE IN BERK...
THE DRAGONS SLEEP COSILY...
AND THEN...

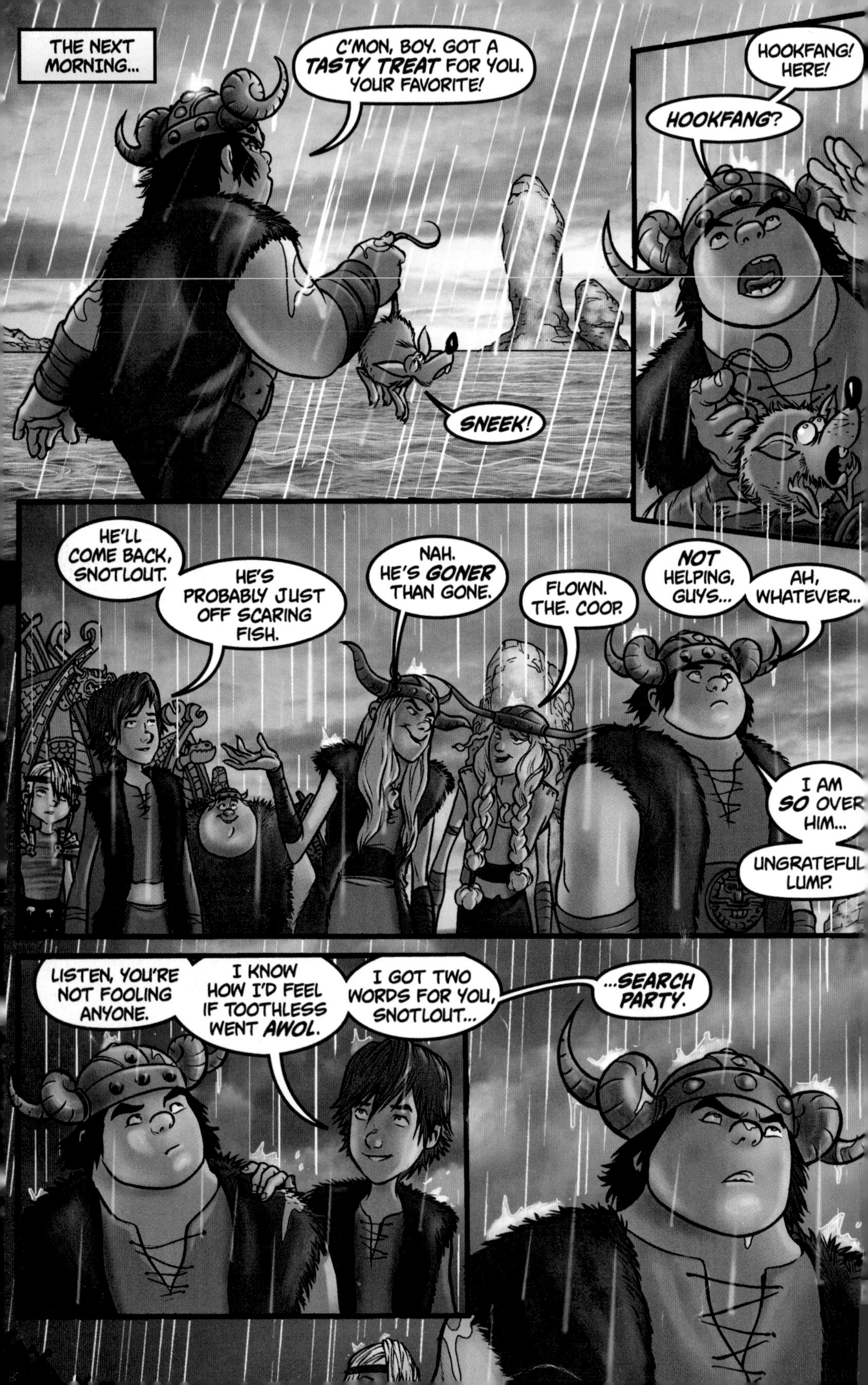

THE NEXT MORNING...
C'MON, BOY. GOT A TASTY TREAT FOR YOU. YOUR FAVORITE!
SNEEK!
HOOKFANG?
HOOKFANG! HERE!
HE'LL COME BACK, SNOTLOUT.
HE'S PROBABLY JUST OFF SCARING FISH.
NAH. HE'S GONER THAN GONE.
FLOWN. THE. COOP.
NOT HELPING, GUYS...
AH, WHATEVER...
I AM SO OVER HIM...
UNGRATEFUL LUMP.
LISTEN, YOU'RE NOT FOOLING ANYONE.
I KNOW HOW I'D FEEL IF TOOTHLESS WENT AWOL.
I GOT TWO WORDS FOR YOU, SNOTLOUT...
...SEARCH PARTY.

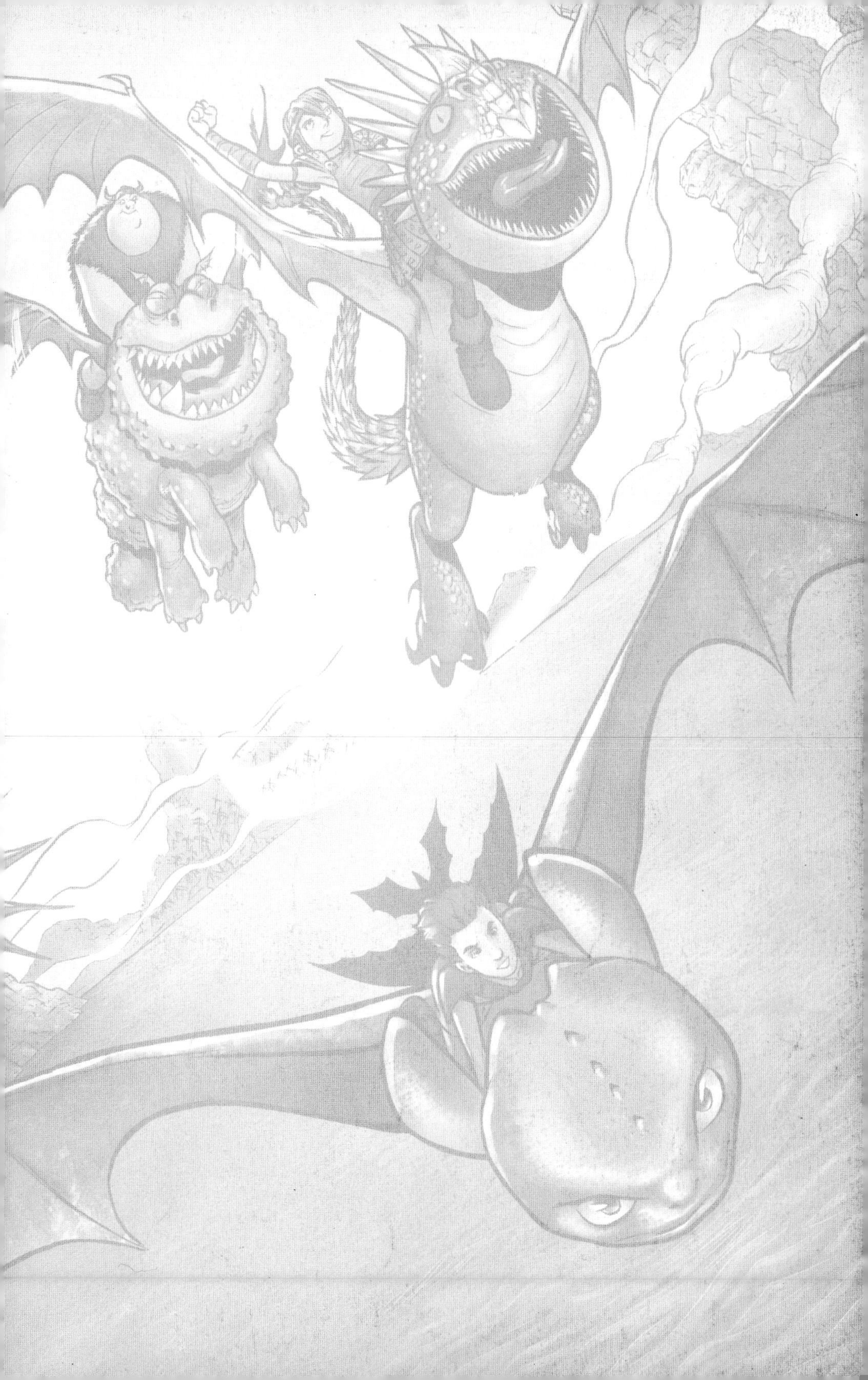

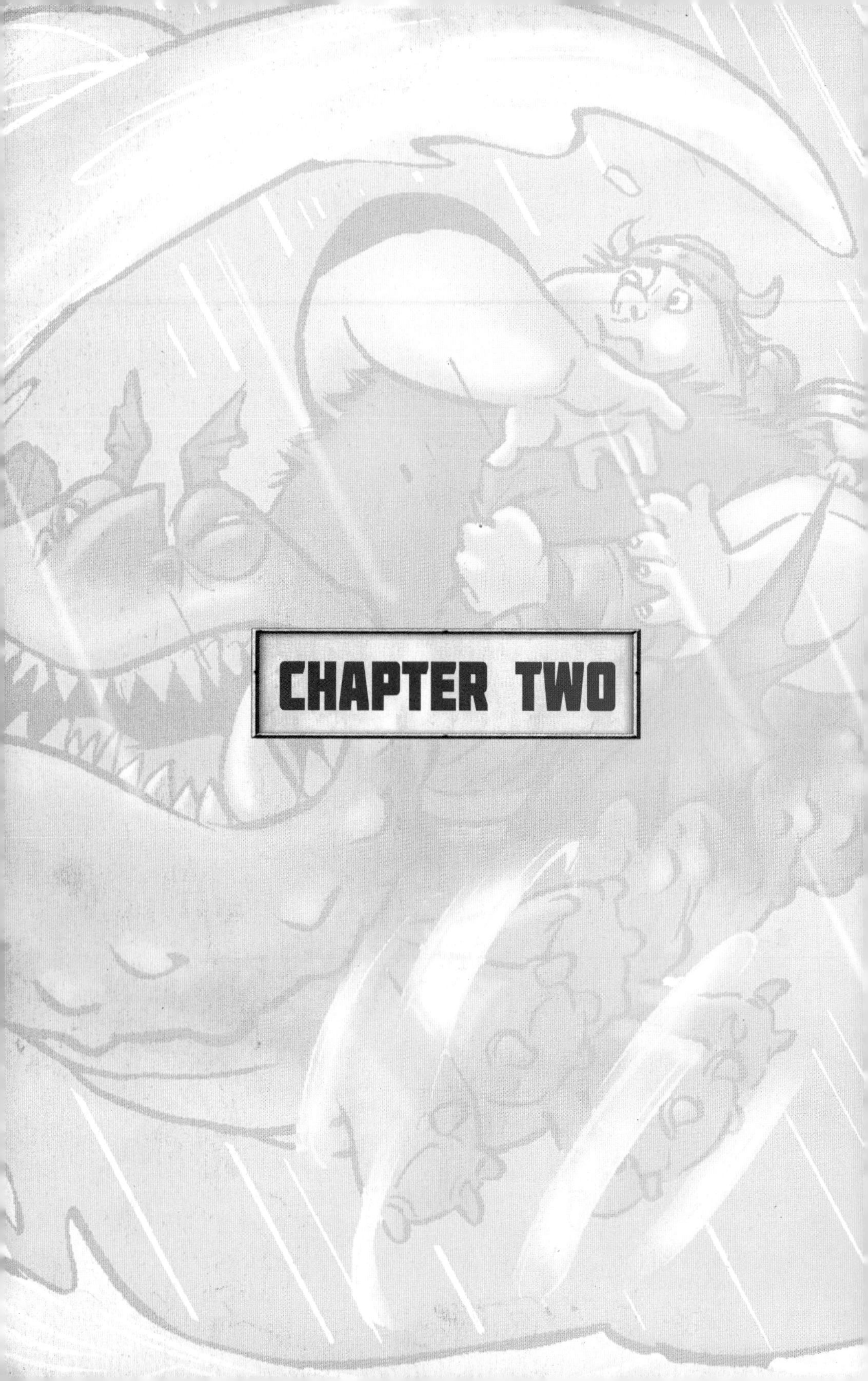

CHAPTER TWO

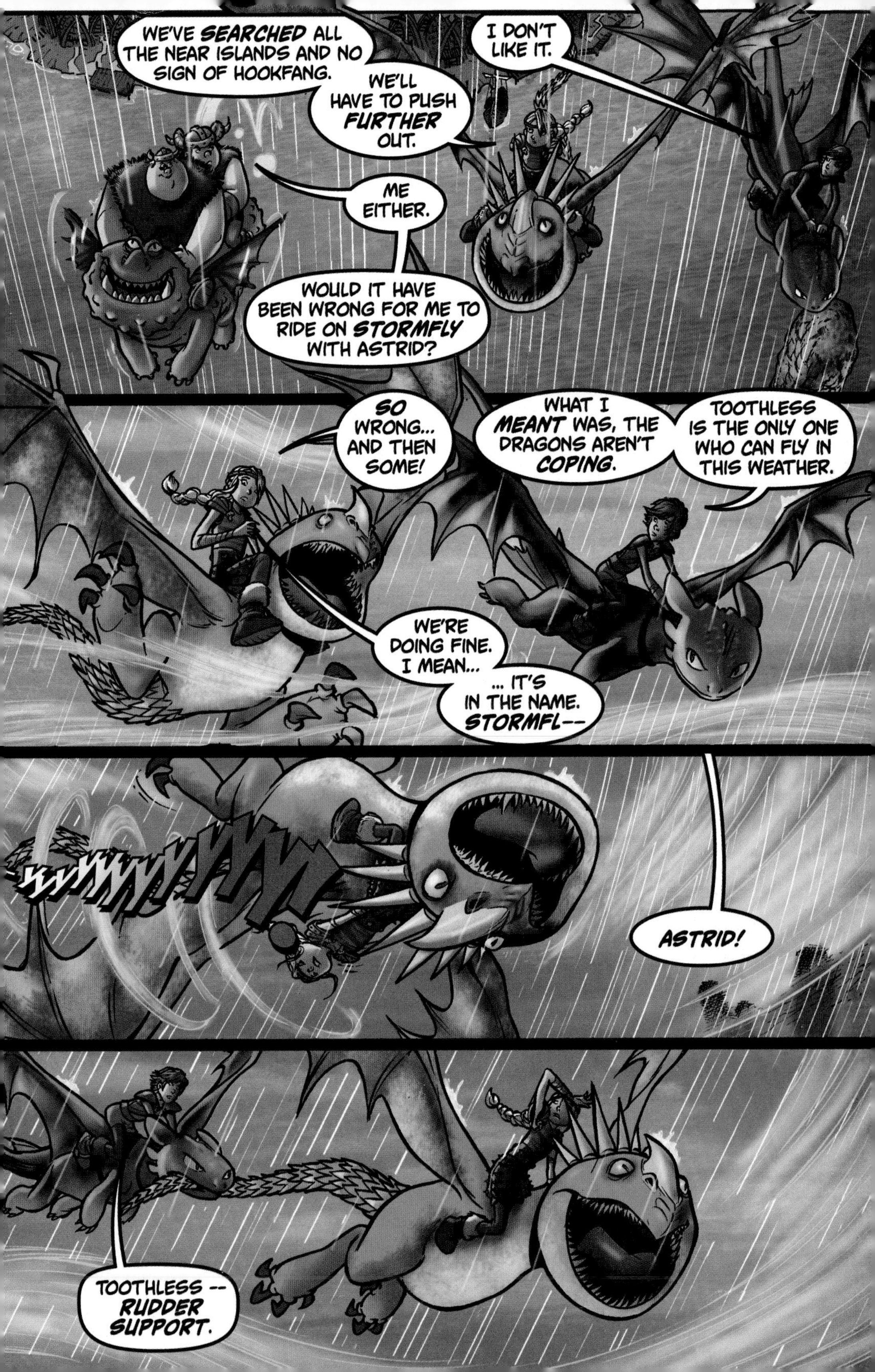
WE'VE SEARCHED ALL THE NEAR ISLANDS AND NO SIGN OF HOOKFANG.
I DON'T LIKE IT.
WE'LL HAVE TO PUSH FURTHER OUT.
ME EITHER.
WOULD IT HAVE BEEN WRONG FOR ME TO RIDE ON STORMFLY WITH ASTRID?
SO WRONG... AND THEN SOME!
WHAT I MEANT WAS, THE DRAGONS AREN'T COPING.
TOOTHLESS IS THE ONLY ONE WHO CAN FLY IN THIS WEATHER.
WE'RE DOING FINE. I MEAN...
... IT'S IN THE NAME. STORMFL--
-YYYWWYYWWW
ASTRID!
TOOTHLESS -- RUDDER SUPPORT.

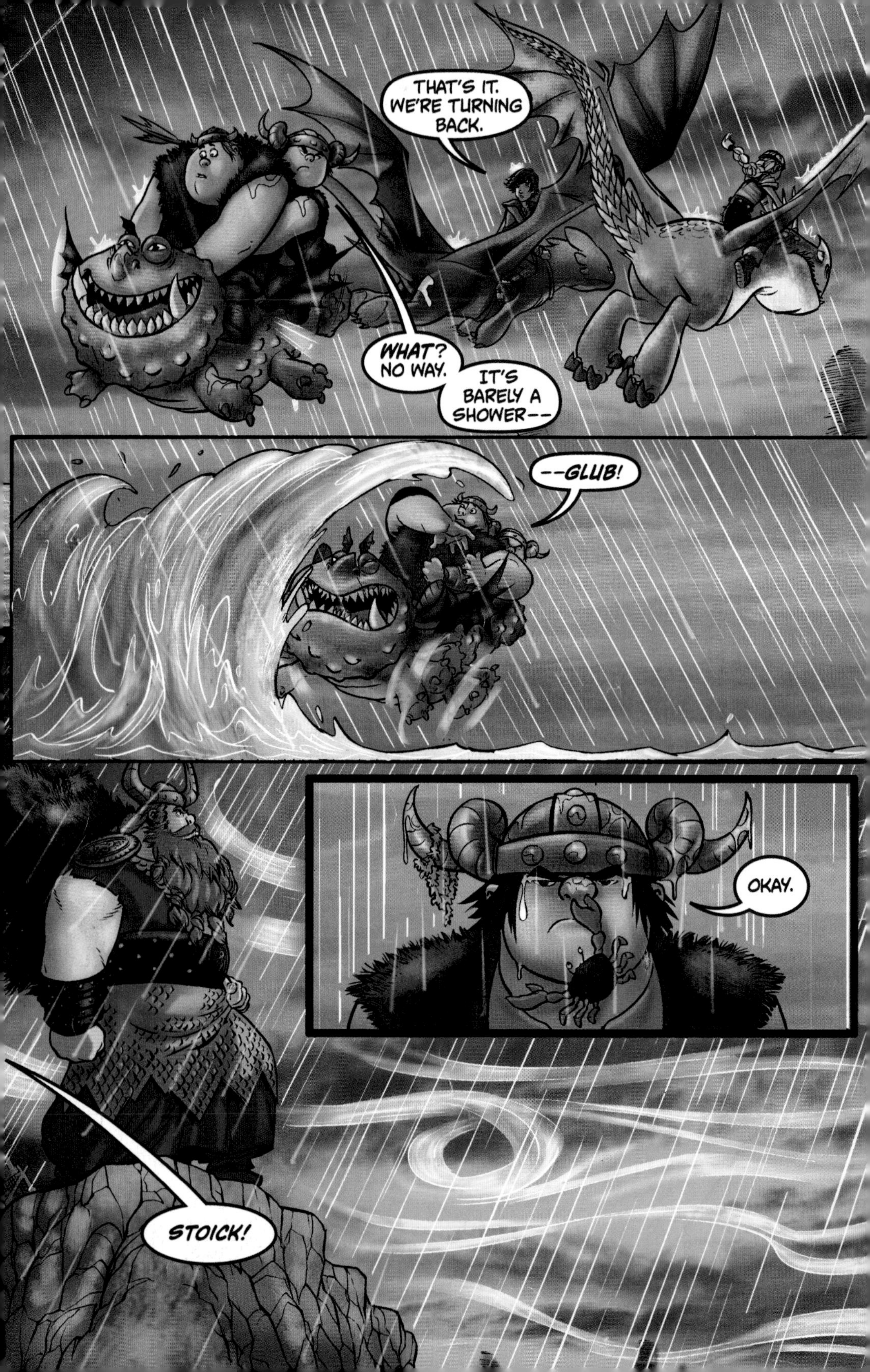
THAT'S IT. WE'RE TURNING BACK.
WHAT? NO WAY.
IT'S BARELY A SHOWER--
--GLUB!
OKAY.
STOICK!

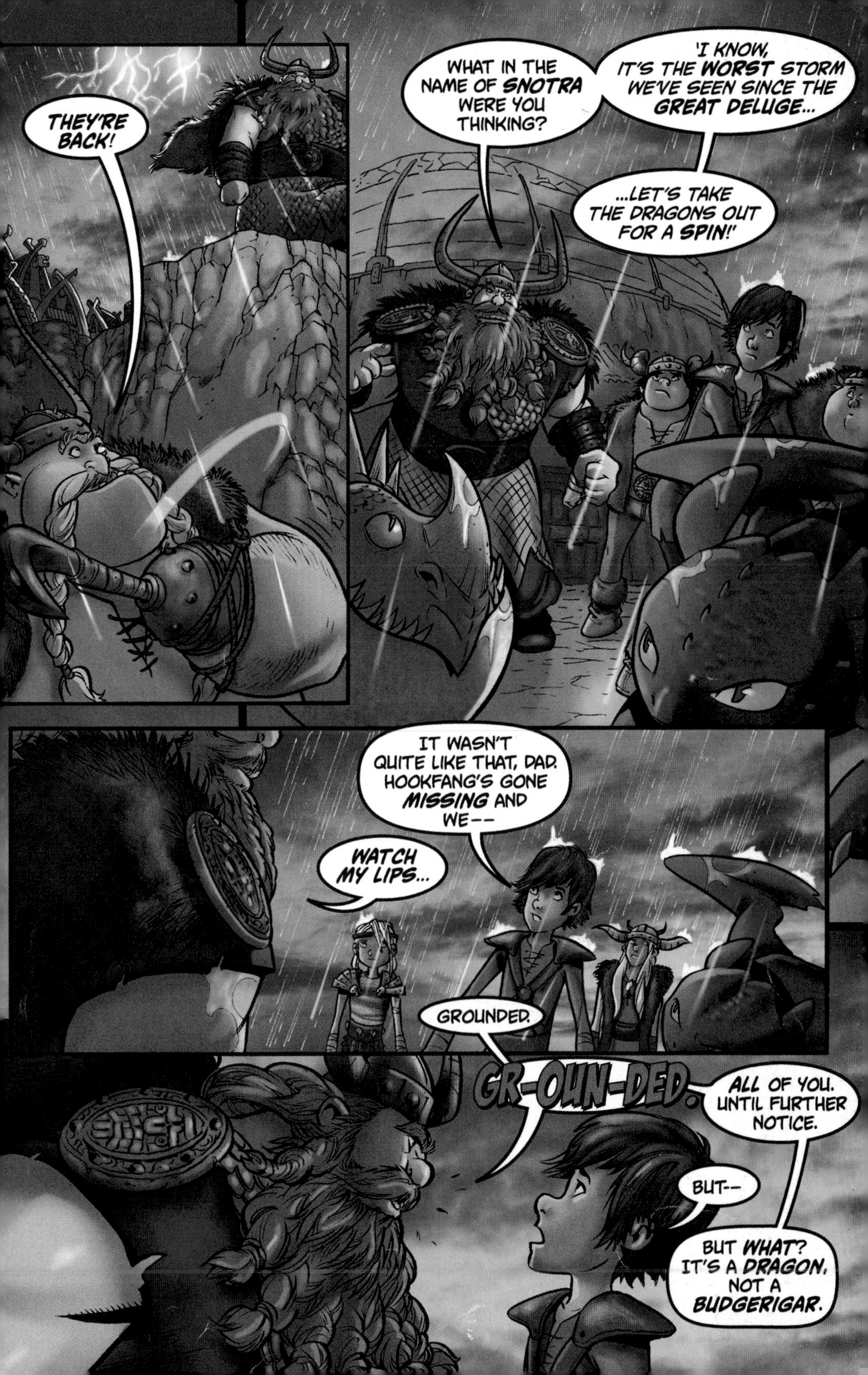
THEY'RE BACK!
WHAT IN THE NAME OF SNOTRA WERE YOU THINKING?
'I KNOW, IT'S THE WORST STORM WE'VE SEEN SINCE THE GREAT DELUGE...
...LET'S TAKE THE DRAGONS OUT FOR A SPIN!'
IT WASN'T QUITE LIKE THAT, DAD. HOOKFANG'S GONE MISSING AND WE--
WATCH MY LIPS...
GROUNDED.
GR-OUN-DED.
ALL OF YOU. UNTIL FURTHER NOTICE.
BUT--
BUT WHAT? IT'S A DRAGON, NOT A BUDGERIGAR.

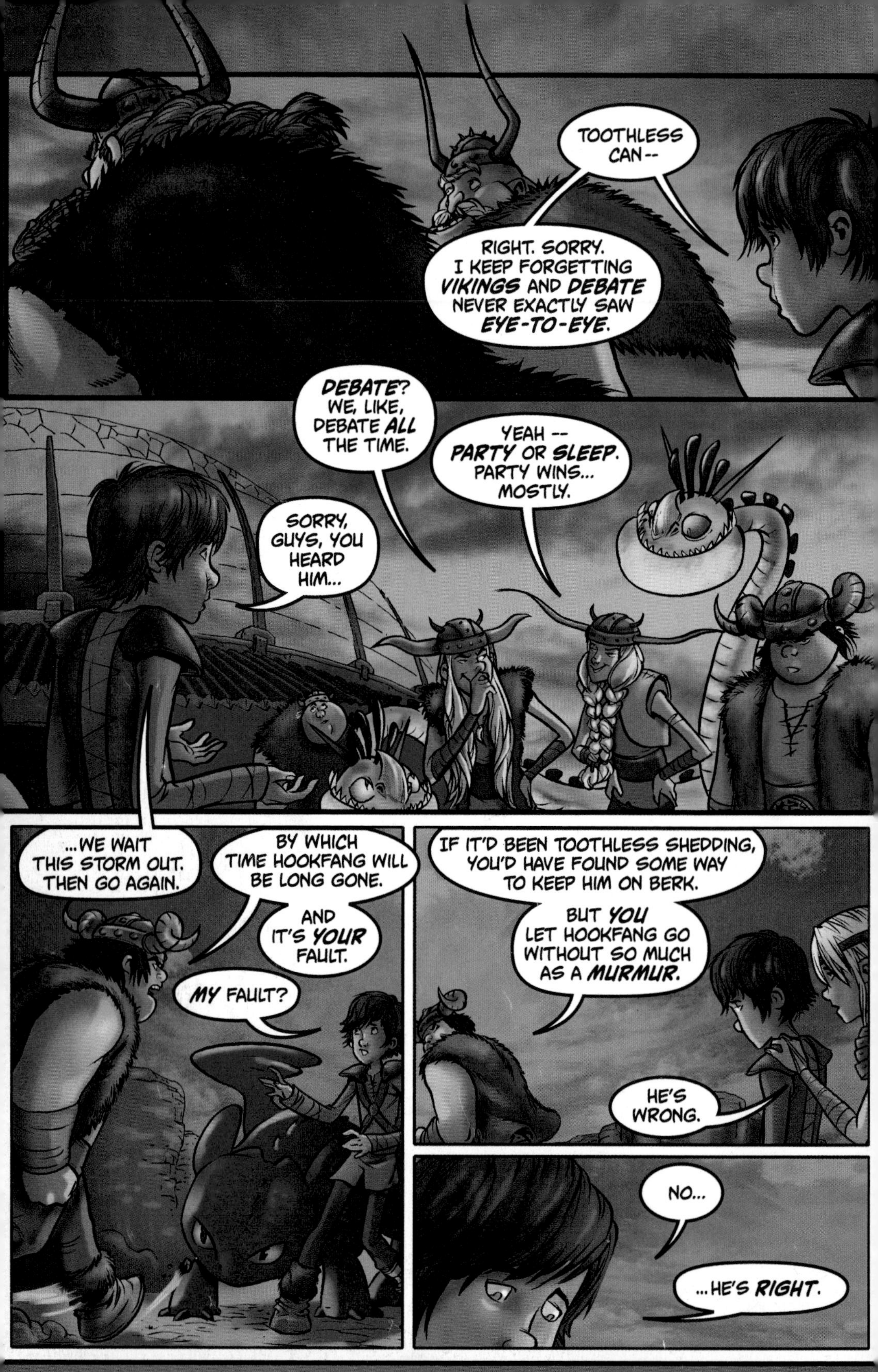
TOOTHLESS CAN--
RIGHT. SORRY. I KEEP FORGETTING *VIKINGS* AND *DEBATE* NEVER EXACTLY SAW *EYE-TO-EYE*.
SORRY, GUYS, YOU HEARD HIM...
DEBATE? WE, LIKE, DEBATE *ALL* THE TIME.
YEAH -- *PARTY* OR *SLEEP*. PARTY WINS... MOSTLY.
...WE WAIT THIS STORM OUT. THEN GO AGAIN.
BY WHICH TIME HOOKFANG WILL BE LONG GONE.
AND IT'S *YOUR* FAULT.
MY FAULT?
IF IT'D BEEN TOOTHLESS SHEDDING, YOU'D HAVE FOUND SOME WAY TO KEEP HIM ON BERK.
BUT *YOU* LET HOOKFANG GO WITHOUT SO MUCH AS A *MURMUR*.
HE'S WRONG.
NO...
...HE'S *RIGHT*.

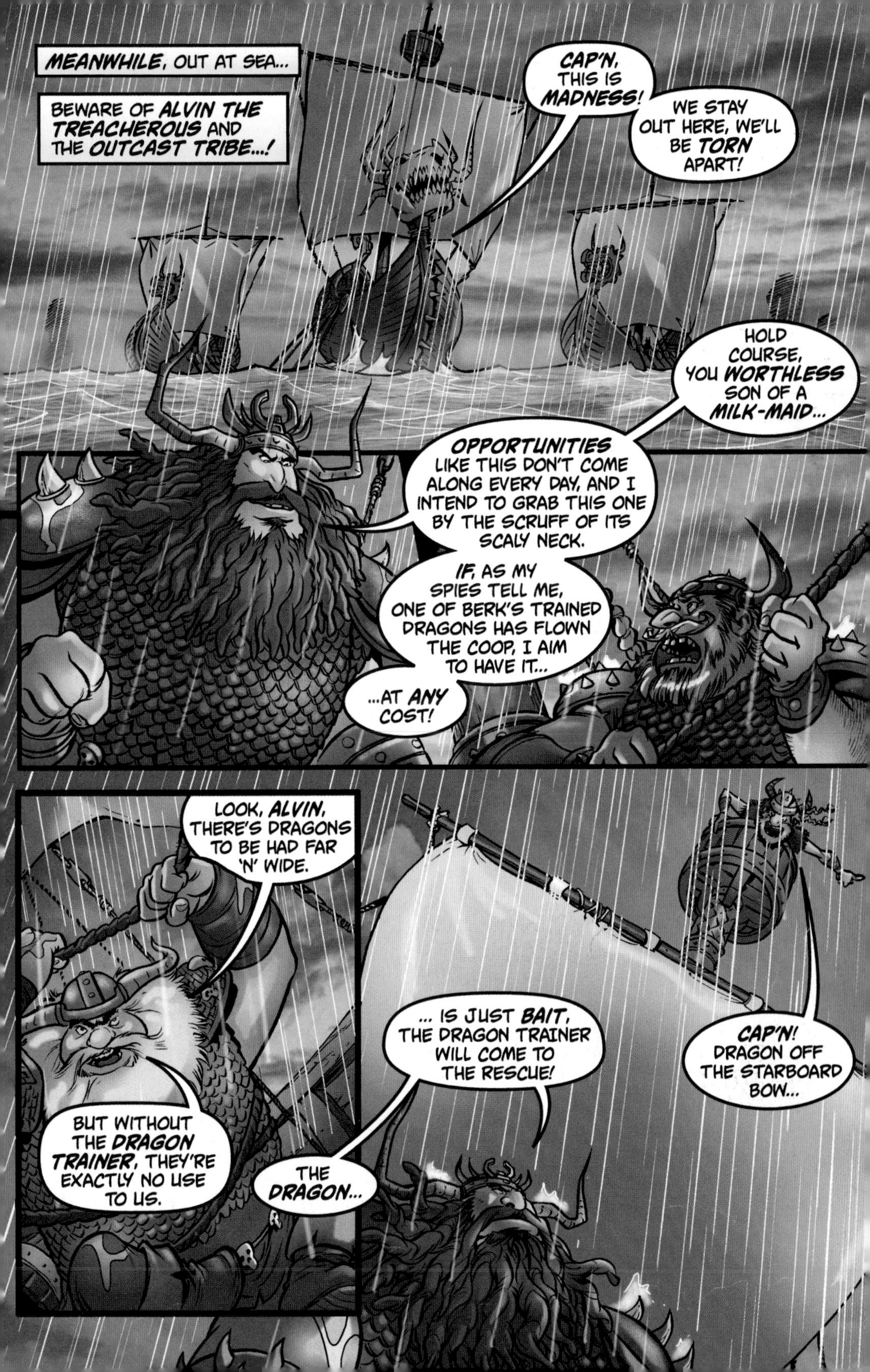
MEANWHILE, OUT AT SEA...
BEWARE OF ALVIN THE TREACHEROUS AND THE OUTCAST TRIBE...!
CAP'N, THIS IS MADNESS!
WE STAY OUT HERE, WE'LL BE TORN APART!
HOLD COURSE, YOU WORTHLESS SON OF A MILK-MAID...
OPPORTUNITIES LIKE THIS DON'T COME ALONG EVERY DAY, AND I INTEND TO GRAB THIS ONE BY THE SCRUFF OF ITS SCALY NECK.
IF, AS MY SPIES TELL ME, ONE OF BERK'S TRAINED DRAGONS HAS FLOWN THE COOP, I AIM TO HAVE IT...
...AT ANY COST!
LOOK, ALVIN, THERE'S DRAGONS TO BE HAD FAR 'N' WIDE.
BUT WITHOUT THE DRAGON TRAINER, THEY'RE EXACTLY NO USE TO US.
THE DRAGON...
... IS JUST BAIT, THE DRAGON TRAINER WILL COME TO THE RESCUE!
CAP'N! DRAGON OFF THE STARBOARD BOW...

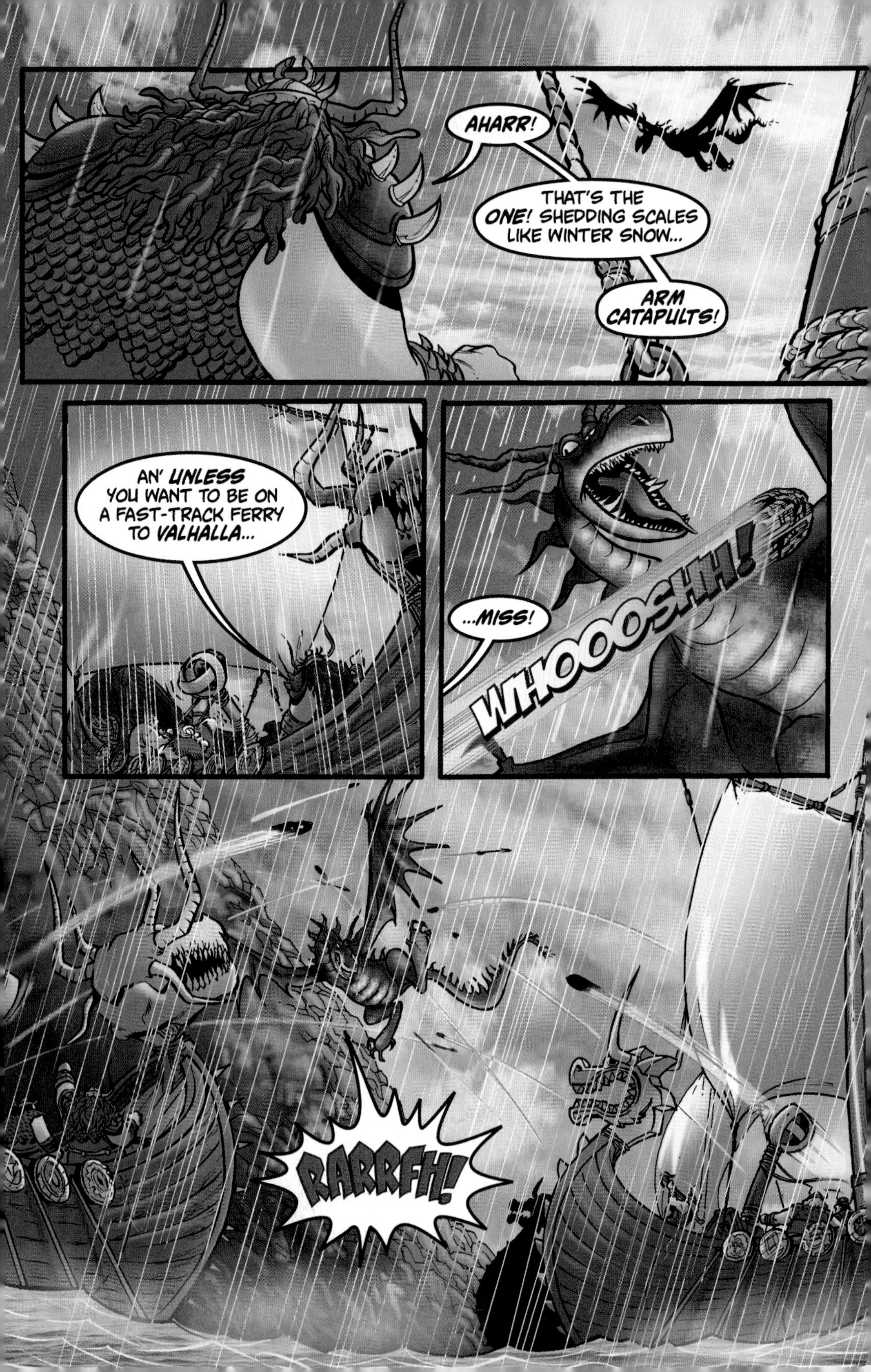
AHARR!
THAT'S THE ONE! SHEDDING SCALES LIKE WINTER SNOW...
ARM CATAPULTS!
AN' UNLESS YOU WANT TO BE ON A FAST-TRACK FERRY TO VALHALLA...
...MISS!
WHOOOOSHH!
RARRFH!

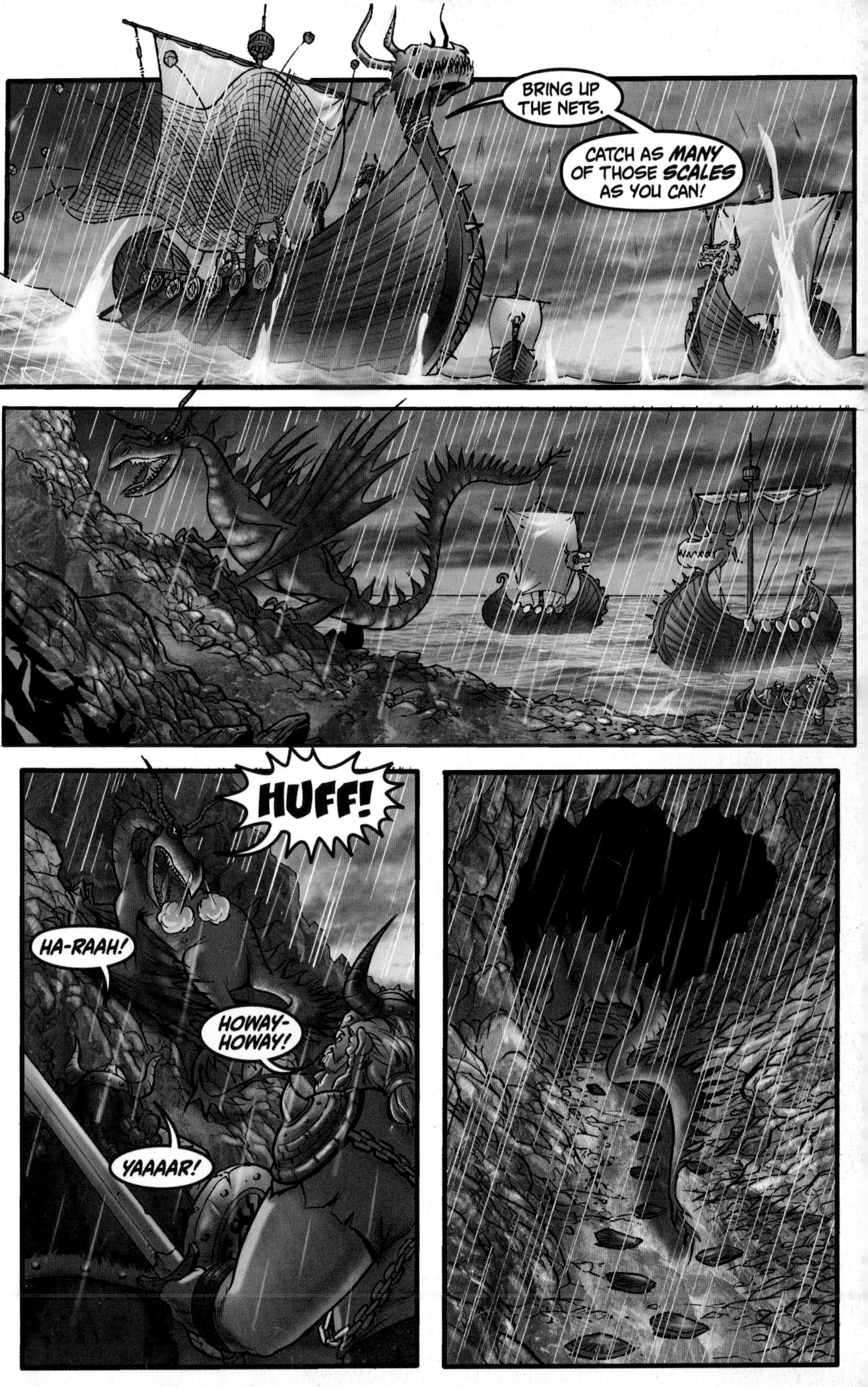
BRING UP THE NETS.
CATCH AS MANY OF THOSE SCALES AS YOU CAN!
HUFF!
HA-RAAH!
HOWAY-HOWAY!
YAAAAR!

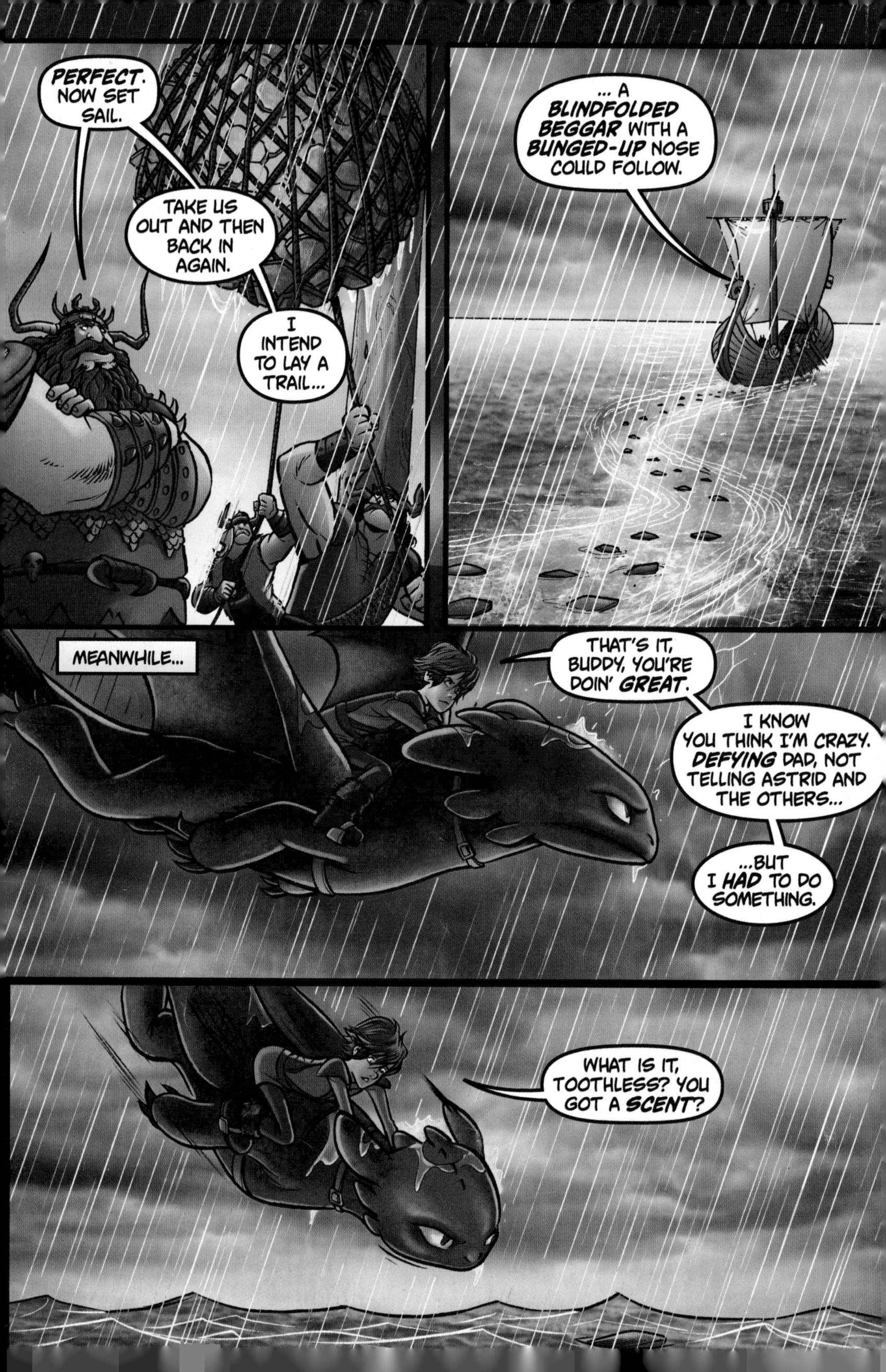
PERFECT. NOW SET SAIL.
TAKE US OUT AND THEN BACK IN AGAIN.
I INTEND TO LAY A TRAIL...
... A BLINDFOLDED BEGGAR WITH A BUNGED-UP NOSE COULD FOLLOW.
MEANWHILE...
THAT'S IT, BUDDY, YOU'RE DOIN' GREAT.
I KNOW YOU THINK I'M CRAZY. DEFYING DAD, NOT TELLING ASTRID AND THE OTHERS...
...BUT I HAD TO DO SOMETHING.
WHAT IS IT, TOOTHLESS? YOU GOT A SCENT?

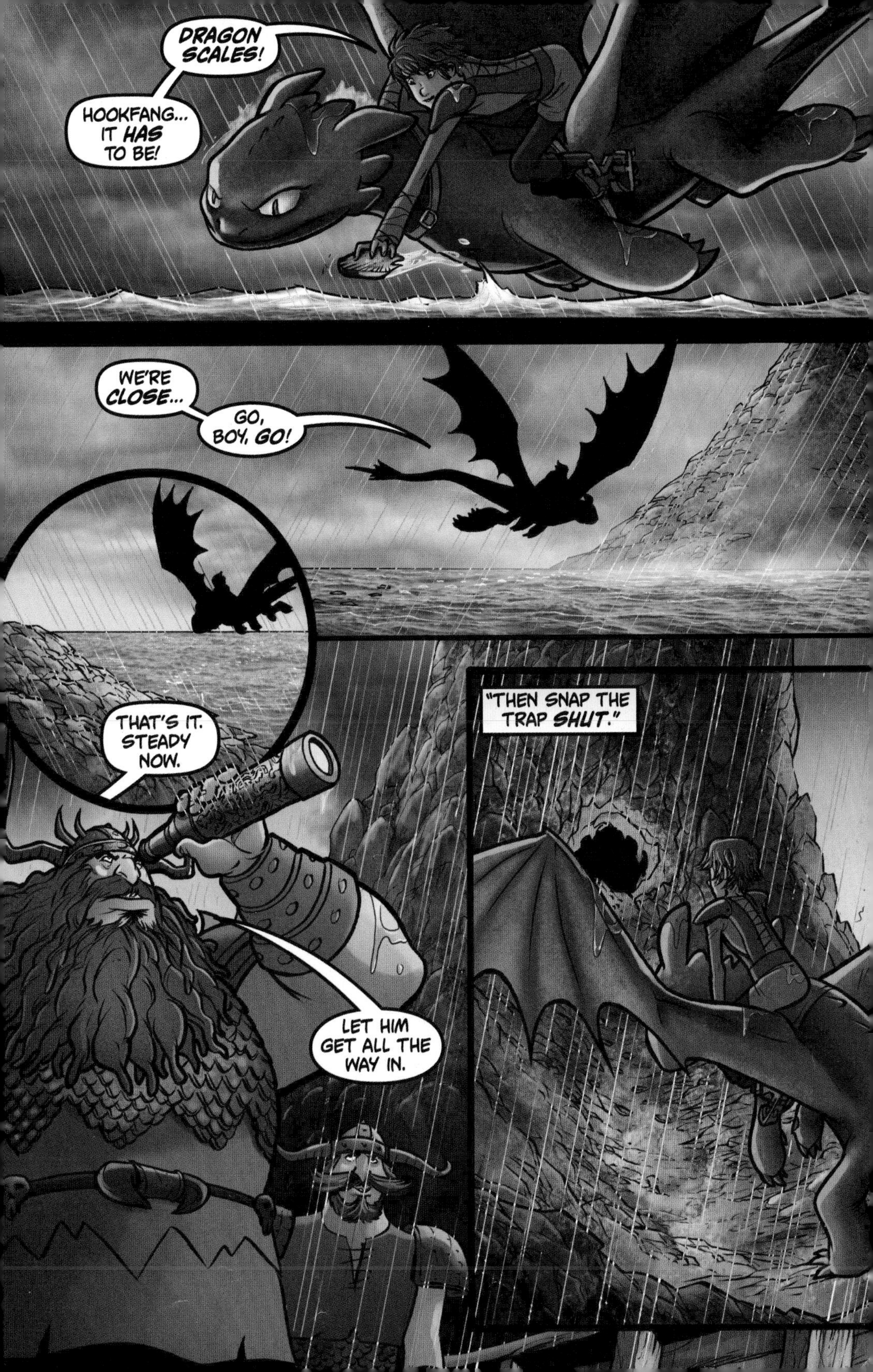
DRAGON SCALES!
HOOKFANG... IT HAS TO BE!
WE'RE CLOSE...
GO, BOY, GO!
THAT'S IT. STEADY NOW.
LET HIM GET ALL THE WAY IN.
"THEN SNAP THE TRAP SHUT."

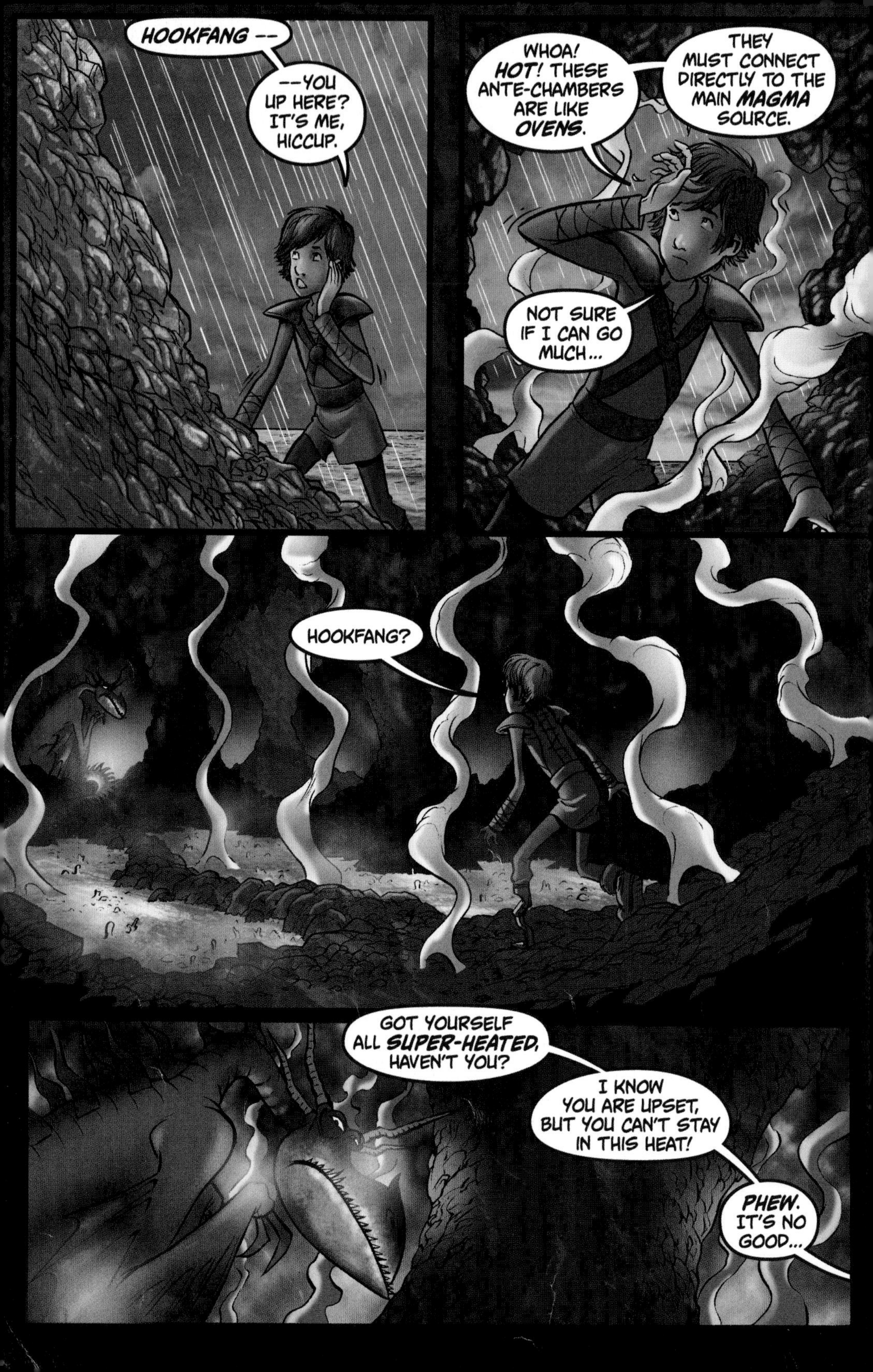
HOOKFANG --
--YOU UP HERE? IT'S ME, HICCUP.
WHOA! HOT! THESE ANTE-CHAMBERS ARE LIKE OVENS.
THEY MUST CONNECT DIRECTLY TO THE MAIN MAGMA SOURCE.
NOT SURE IF I CAN GO MUCH...
HOOKFANG?
GOT YOURSELF ALL SUPER-HEATED, HAVEN'T YOU?
I KNOW YOU ARE UPSET, BUT YOU CAN'T STAY IN THIS HEAT!
PHEW. IT'S NO GOOD...

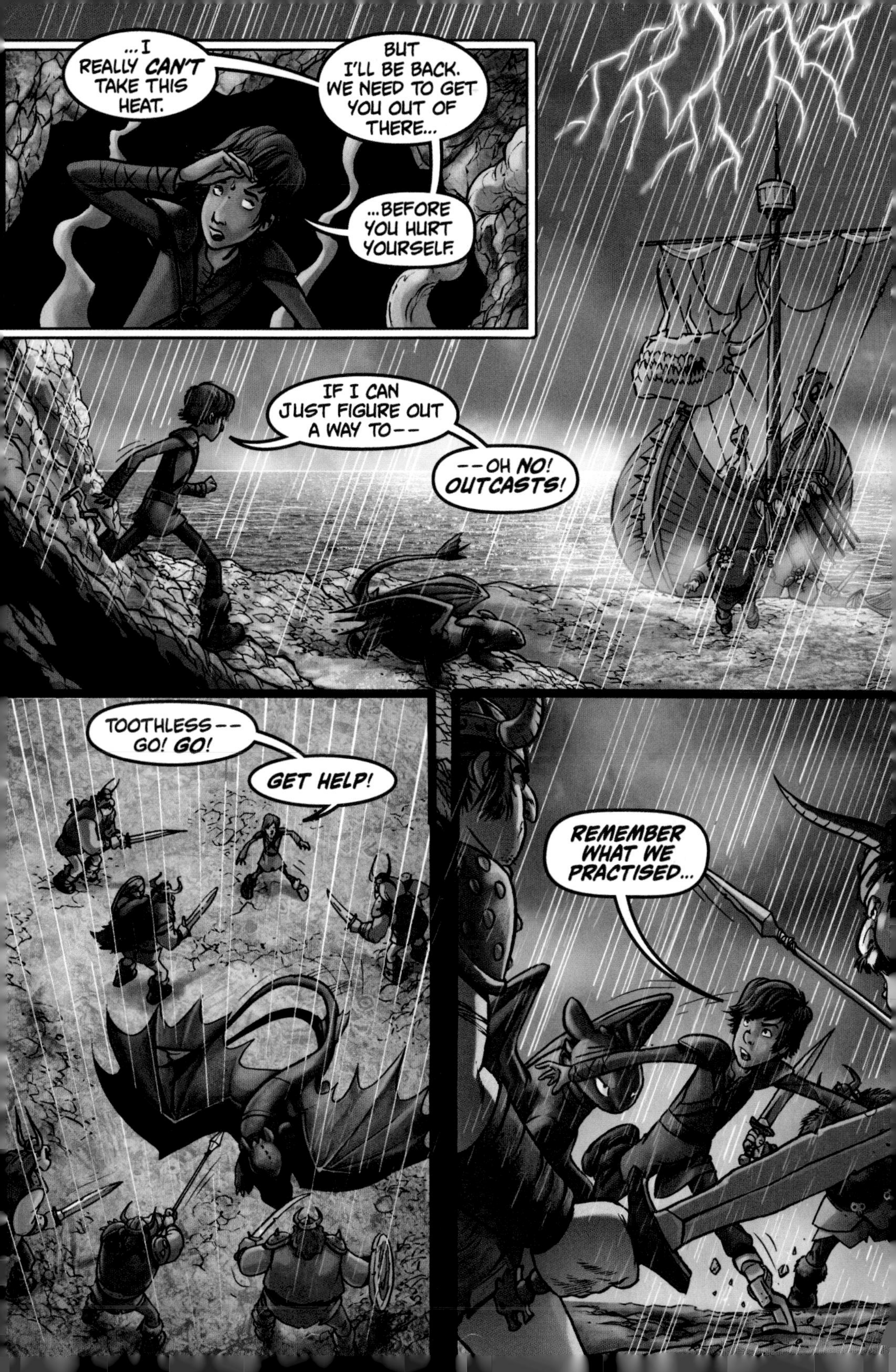
...I REALLY CAN'T TAKE THIS HEAT.
BUT I'LL BE BACK. WE NEED TO GET YOU OUT OF THERE...
...BEFORE YOU HURT YOURSELF.
IF I CAN JUST FIGURE OUT A WAY TO--
--OH NO! OUTCASTS!
TOOTHLESS-- GO! GO!
GET HELP!
REMEMBER WHAT WE PRACTISED...

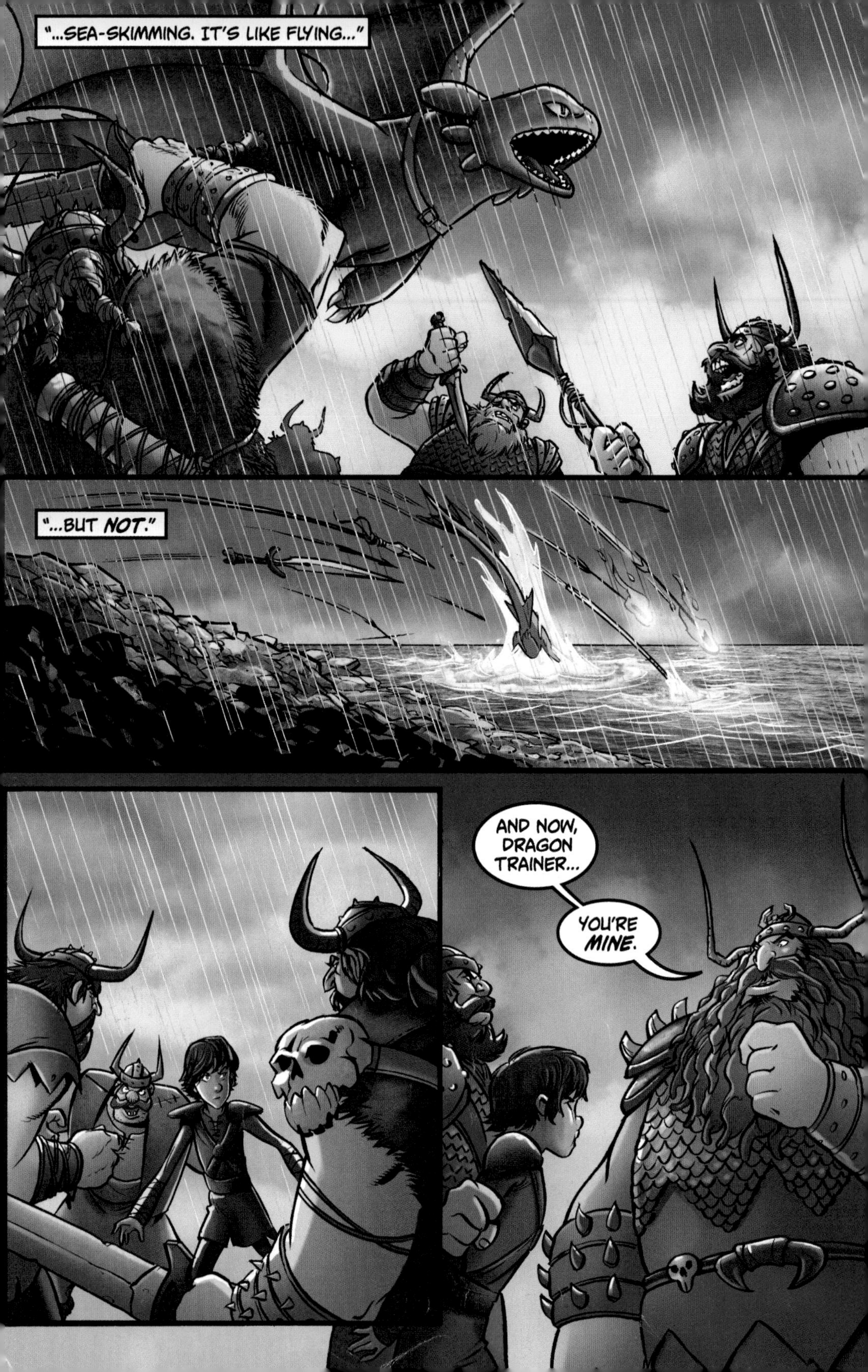
"...SEA-SKIMMING. IT'S LIKE FLYING..."
"...BUT NOT."
AND NOW, DRAGON TRAINER...
YOU'RE MINE.

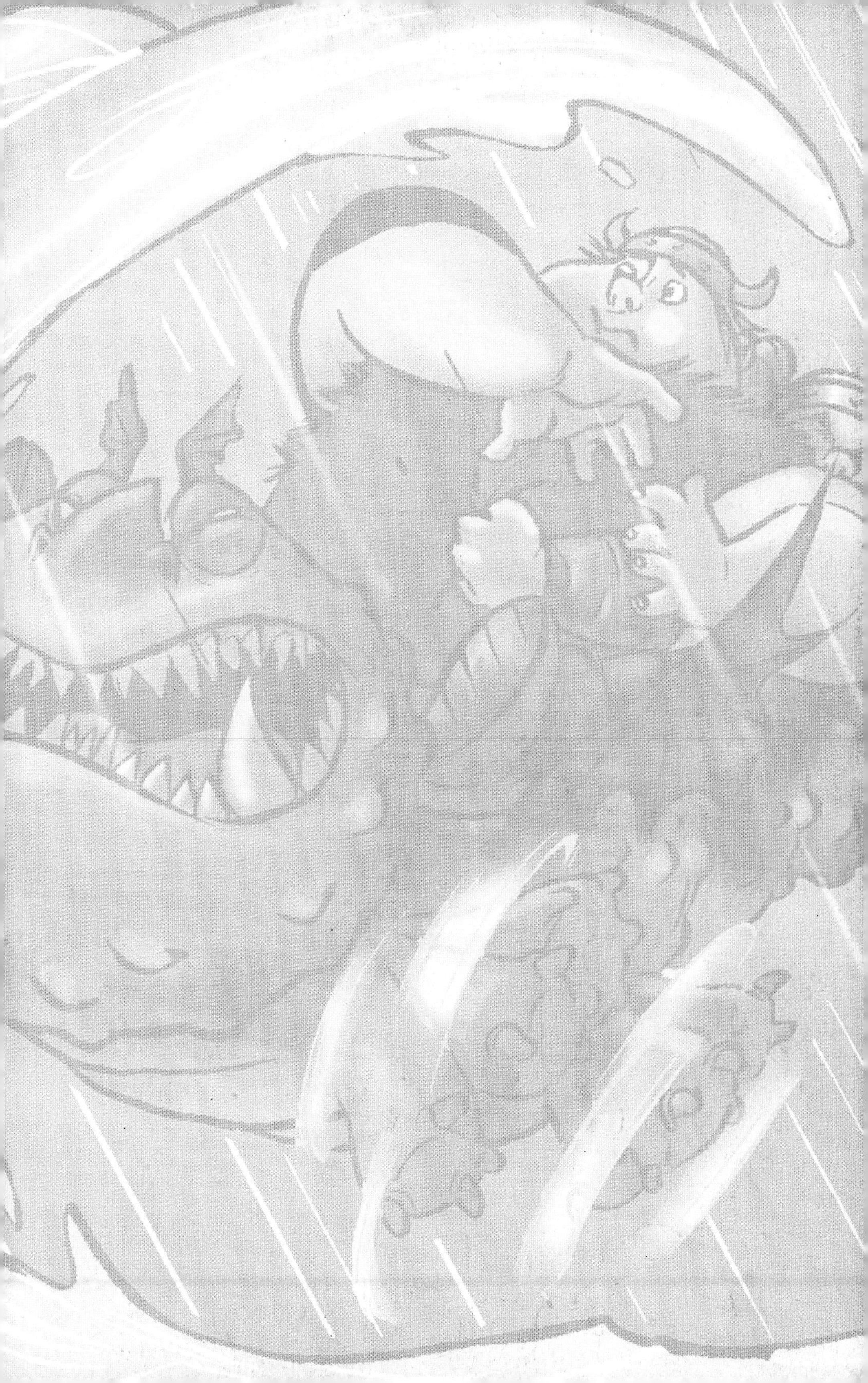

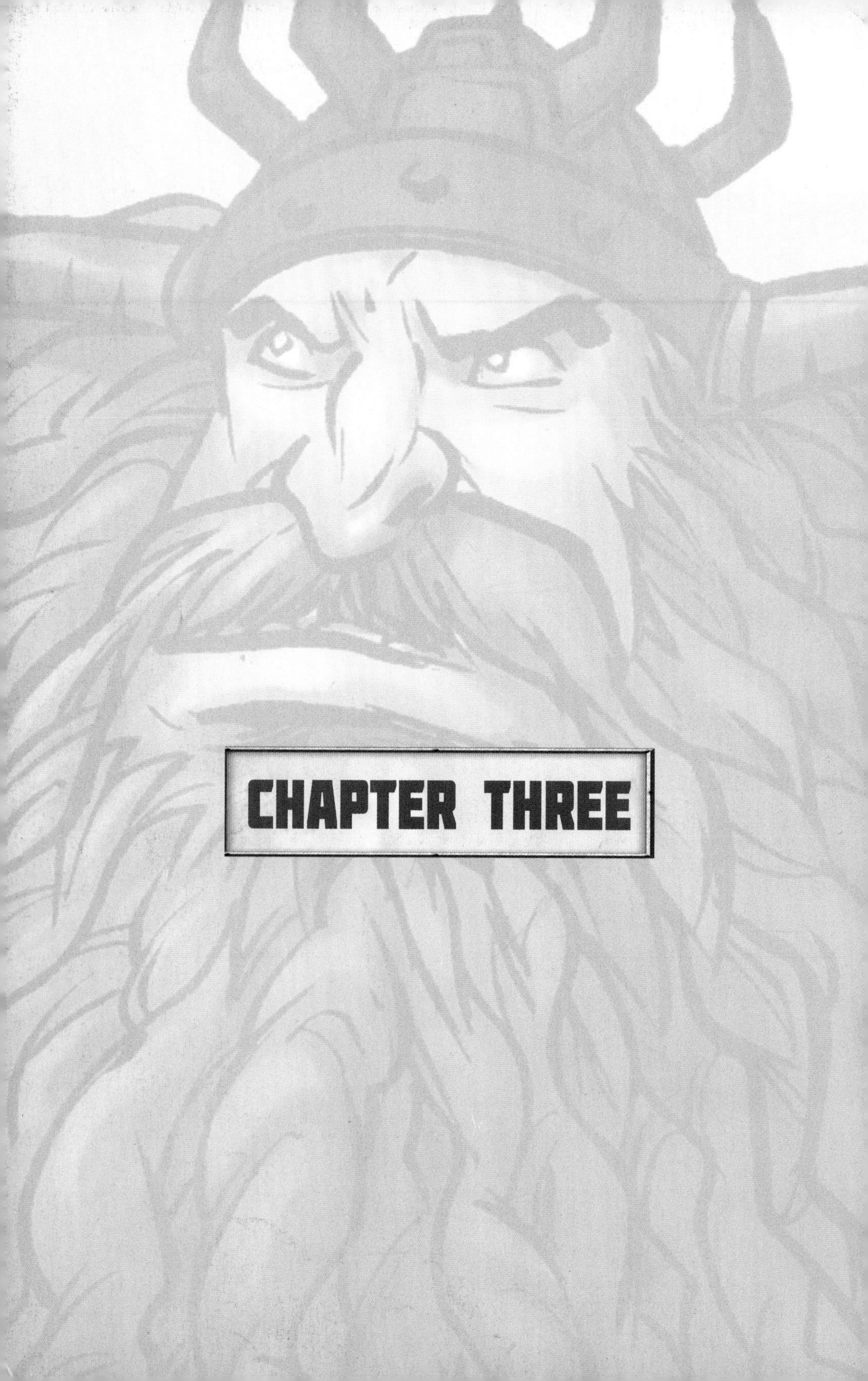

CHAPTER THREE

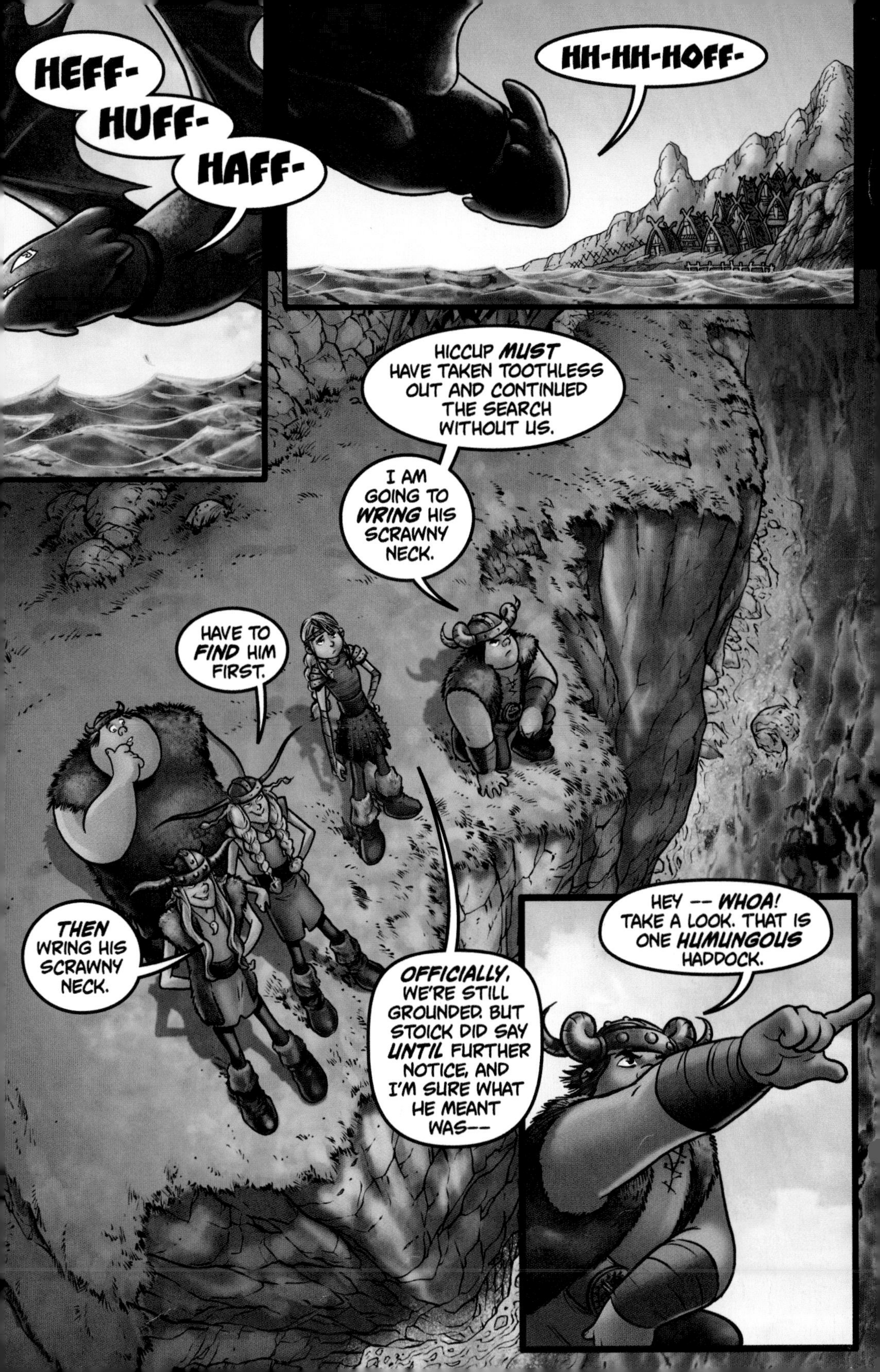
HEFF-
HUFF-
HAFF-
HH-HH-HOFF-
HICCUP MUST HAVE TAKEN TOOTHLESS OUT AND CONTINUED THE SEARCH WITHOUT US.
I AM GOING TO WRING HIS SCRAWNY NECK.
HAVE TO FIND HIM FIRST.
THEN WRING HIS SCRAWNY NECK.
OFFICIALLY, WE'RE STILL GROUNDED. BUT STOICK DID SAY UNTIL FURTHER NOTICE, AND I'M SURE WHAT HE MEANT WAS--
HEY -- WHOA! TAKE A LOOK. THAT IS ONE HUMUNGOUS HADDOCK.

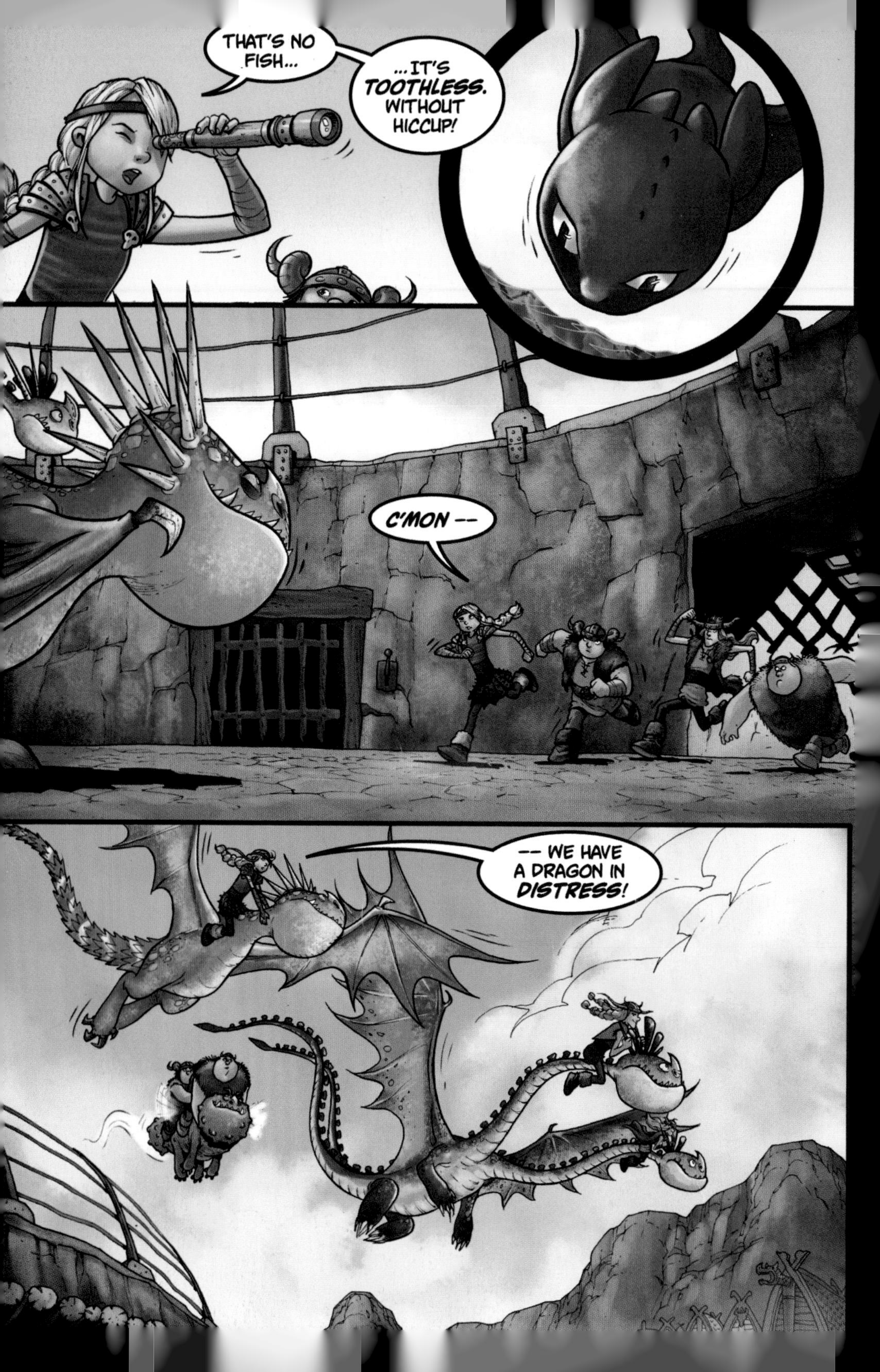
THAT'S NO FISH...
...IT'S TOOTHLESS. WITHOUT HICCUP!
C'MON --
-- WE HAVE A DRAGON IN DISTRESS!

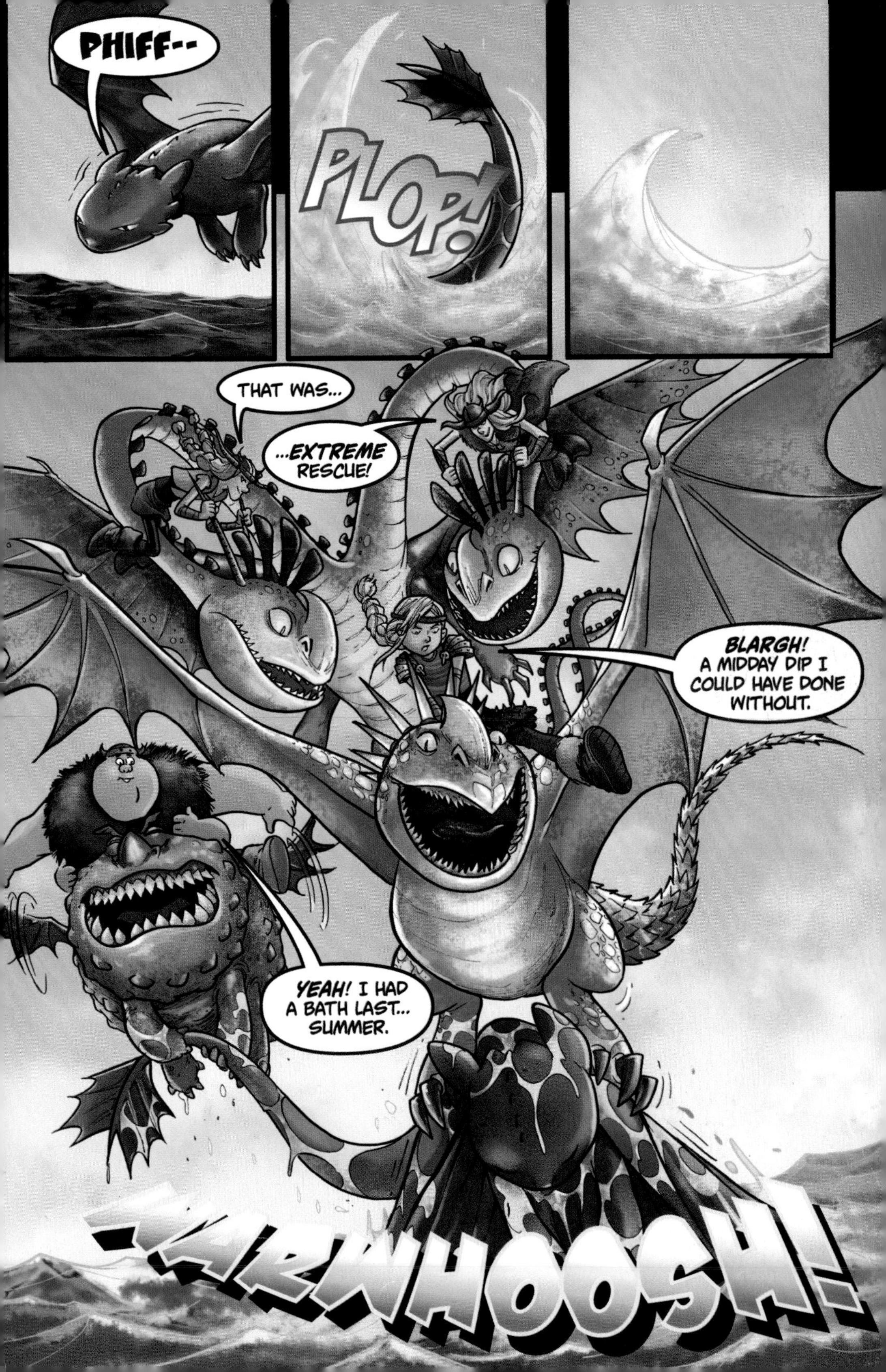
PHIFF--
PLOP!
THAT WAS...
...EXTREME RESCUE!
BLARGH! A MIDDAY DIP I COULD HAVE DONE WITHOUT.
YEAH! I HAD A BATH LAST... SUMMER.
WHOOSH!

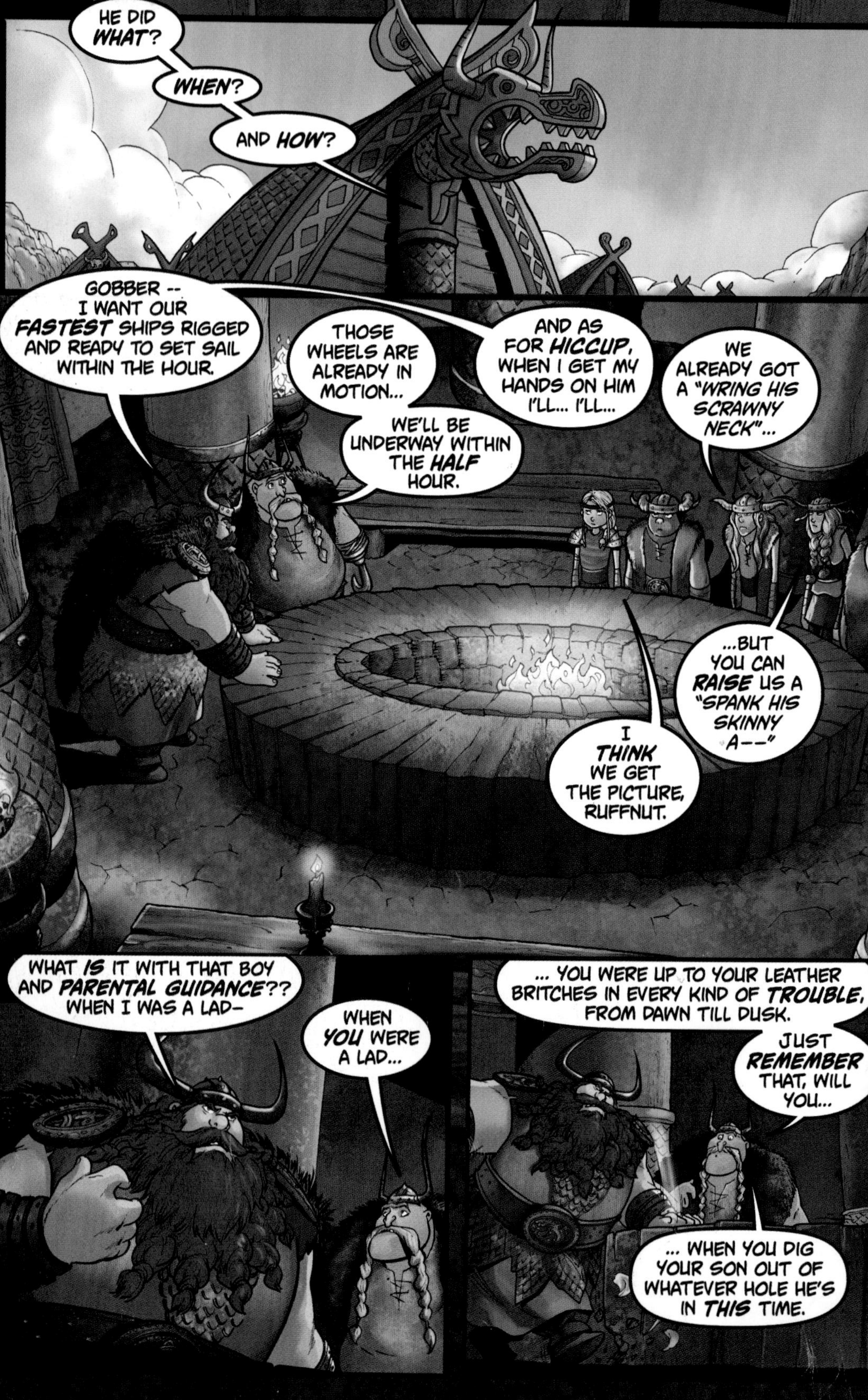

HE DID WHAT?
WHEN?
AND HOW?
GOBBER -- I WANT OUR FASTEST SHIPS RIGGED AND READY TO SET SAIL WITHIN THE HOUR.
THOSE WHEELS ARE ALREADY IN MOTION...
WE'LL BE UNDERWAY WITHIN THE HALF HOUR.
AND AS FOR HICCUP, WHEN I GET MY HANDS ON HIM I'LL... I'LL...
WE ALREADY GOT A "WRING HIS SCRAWNY NECK"...
...BUT YOU CAN RAISE US A "SPANK HIS SKINNY A--"
I THINK WE GET THE PICTURE, RUFFNUT.
WHAT IS IT WITH THAT BOY AND PARENTAL GUIDANCE?? WHEN I WAS A LAD-
WHEN YOU WERE A LAD...
... YOU WERE UP TO YOUR LEATHER BRITCHES IN EVERY KIND OF TROUBLE, FROM DAWN TILL DUSK.
JUST REMEMBER THAT, WILL YOU...
... WHEN YOU DIG YOUR SON OUT OF WHATEVER HOLE HE'S IN THIS TIME.

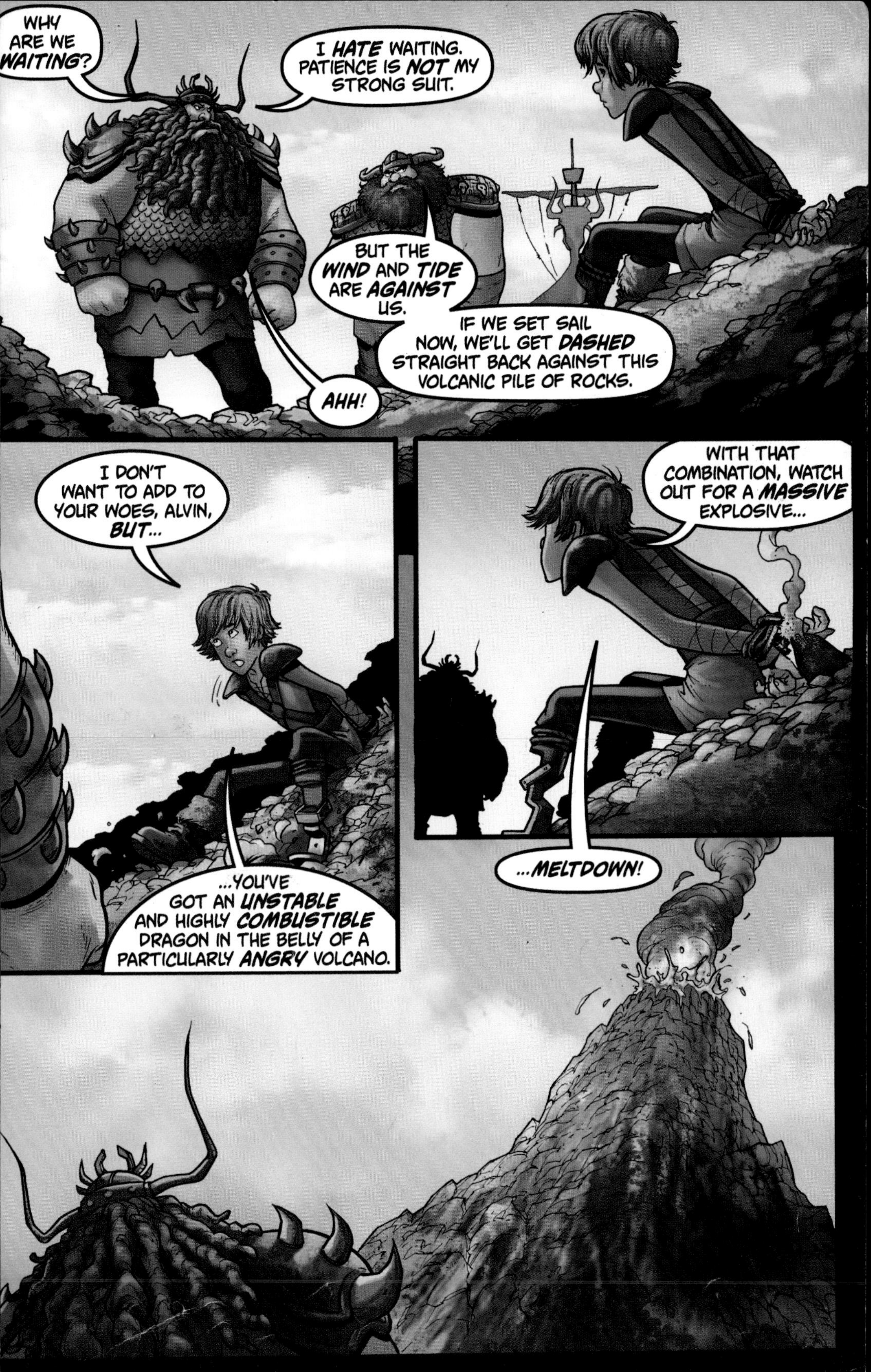
WHY ARE WE WAITING?
I HATE WAITING. PATIENCE IS NOT MY STRONG SUIT.
BUT THE WIND AND TIDE ARE AGAINST US.
IF WE SET SAIL NOW, WE'LL GET DASHED STRAIGHT BACK AGAINST THIS VOLCANIC PILE OF ROCKS.
AHH!
I DON'T WANT TO ADD TO YOUR WOES, ALVIN, BUT...
...YOU'VE GOT AN UNSTABLE AND HIGHLY COMBUSTIBLE DRAGON IN THE BELLY OF A PARTICULARLY ANGRY VOLCANO.
WITH THAT COMBINATION, WATCH OUT FOR A MASSIVE EXPLOSIVE...
...MELTDOWN!

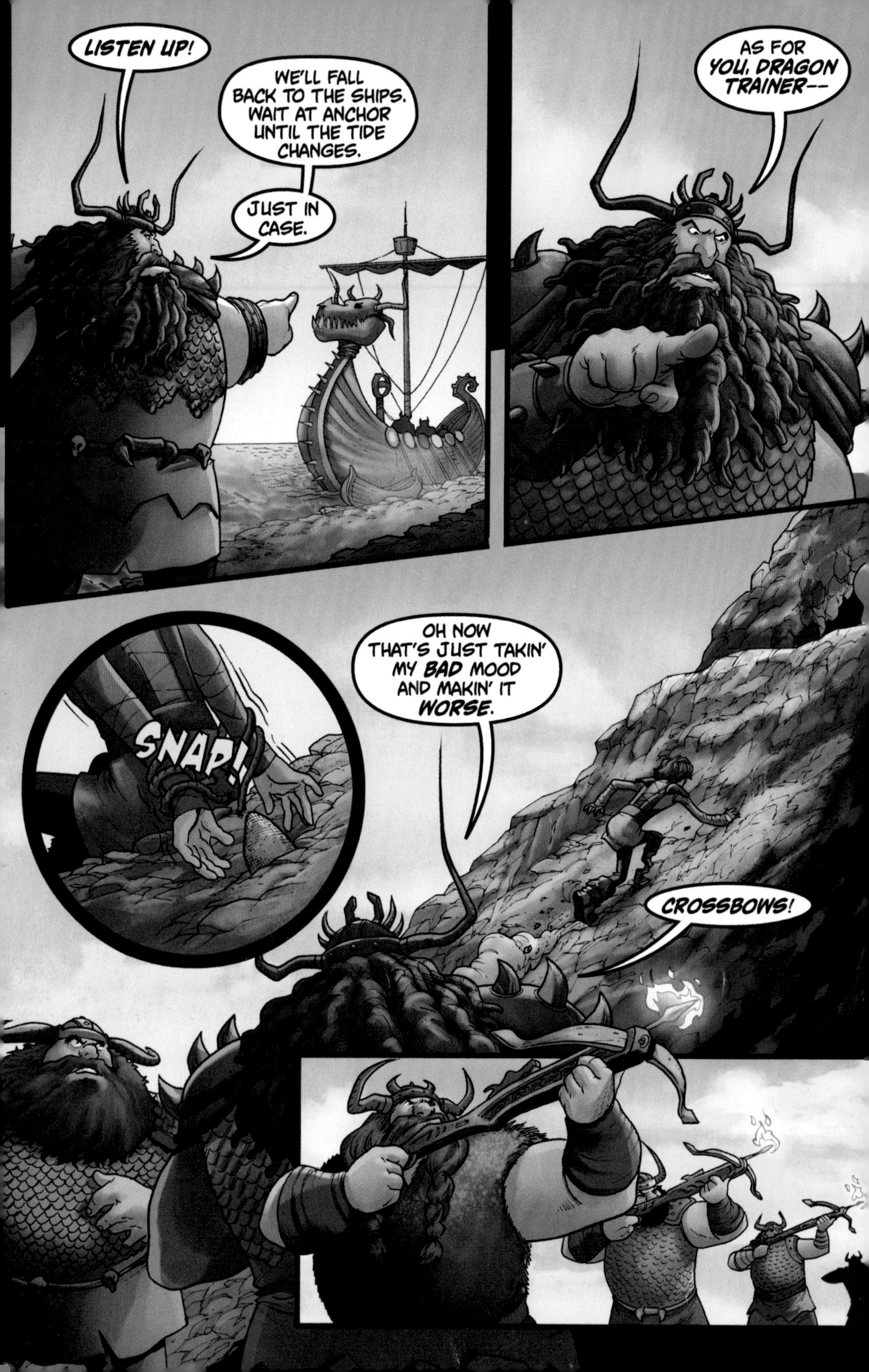
LISTEN UP!
WE'LL FALL BACK TO THE SHIPS. WAIT AT ANCHOR UNTIL THE TIDE CHANGES.
JUST IN CASE.
AS FOR YOU, DRAGON TRAINER--
SNAP!
OH NOW THAT'S JUST TAKIN' MY BAD MOOD AND MAKIN' IT WORSE.
CROSSBOWS!

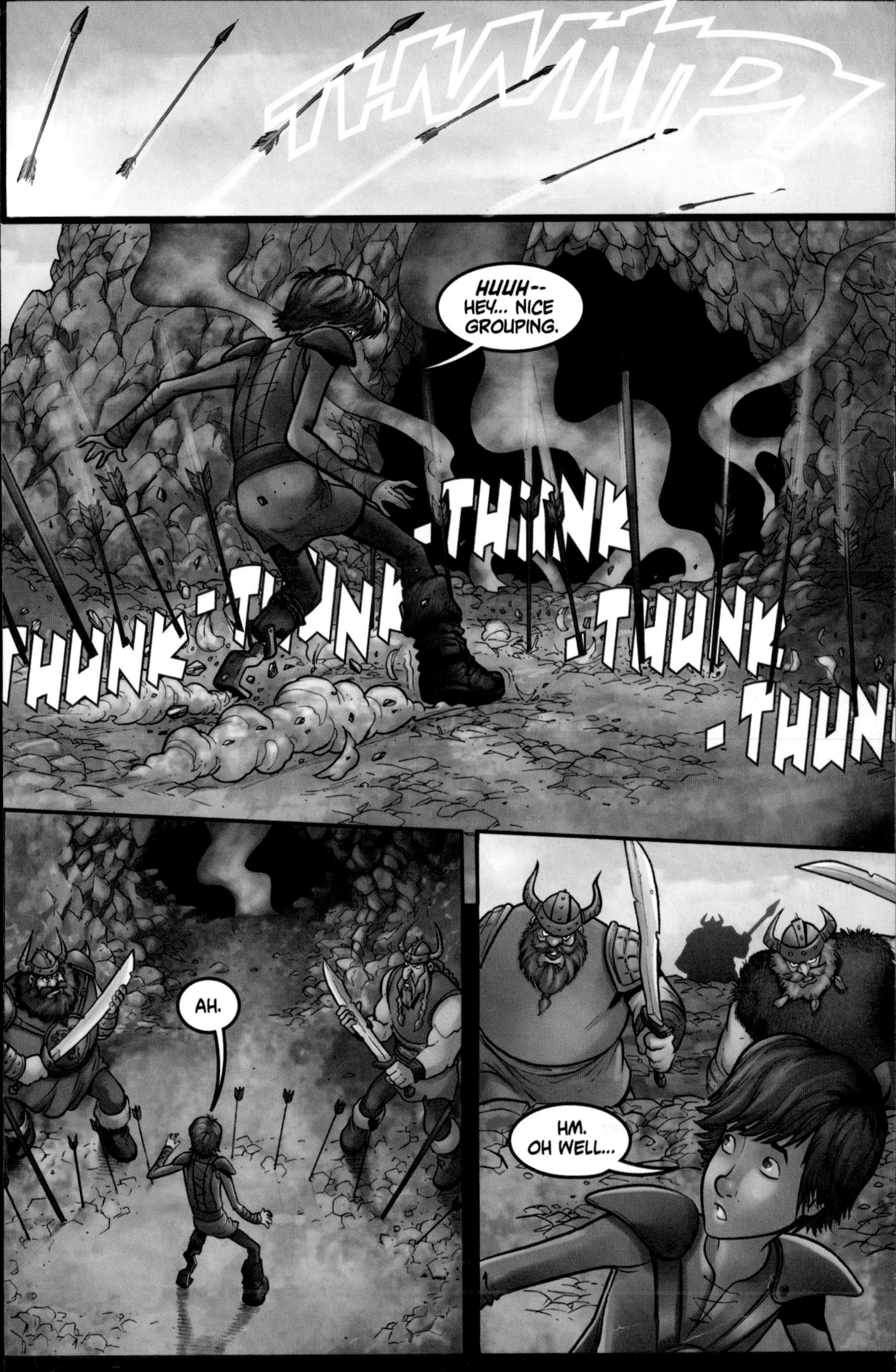
THWWIP
HUUH-- HEY... NICE GROUPING.
THUNK
THUNK
THUNK
THUNK
THUN
AH.
HM. OH WELL...

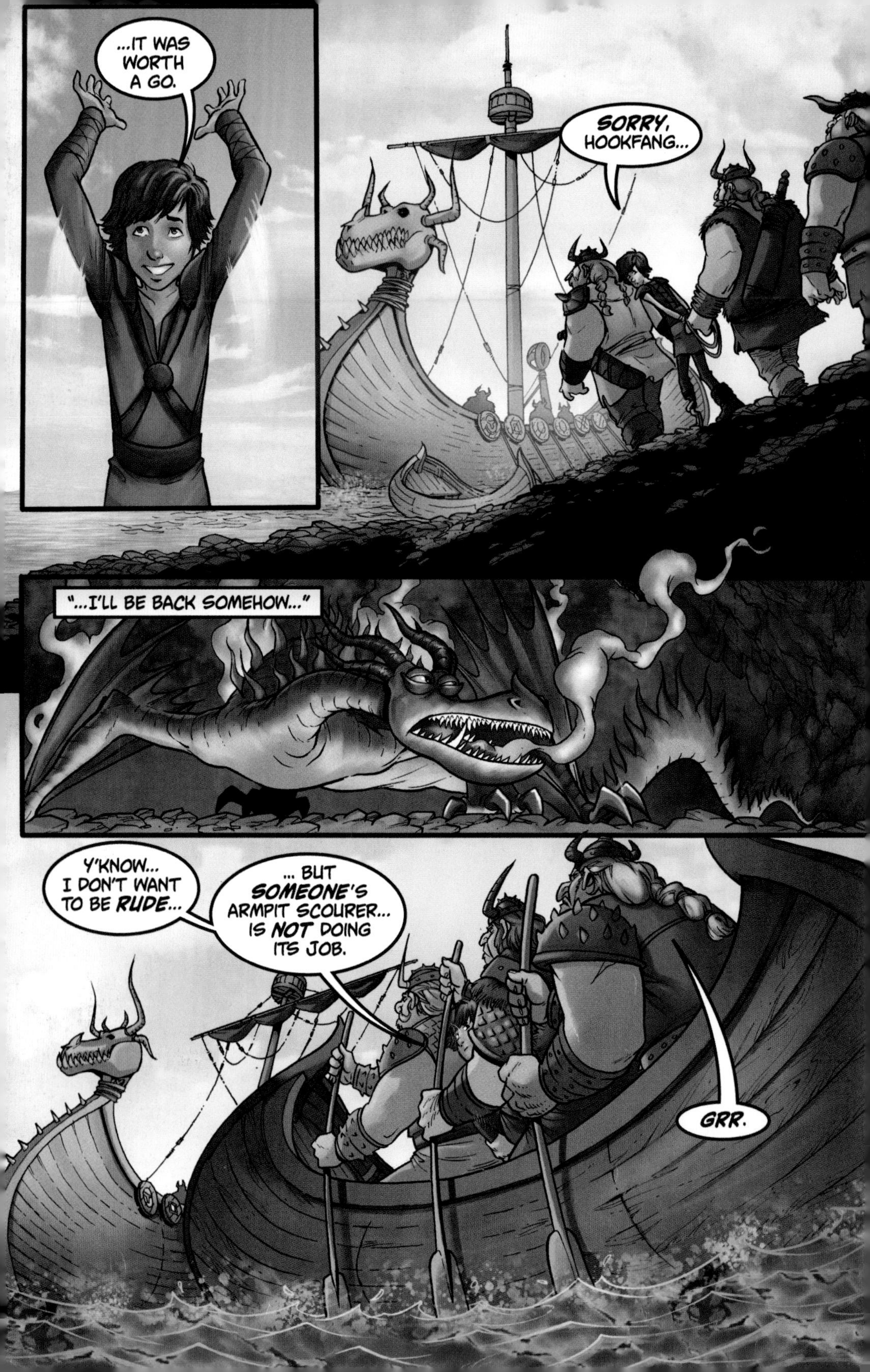
...IT WAS WORTH A GO.
SORRY, HOOKFANG...
"...I'LL BE BACK SOMEHOW..."
Y'KNOW... I DON'T WANT TO BE RUDE...
... BUT SOMEONE'S ARMPIT SCOURER... IS NOT DOING ITS JOB.
GRR.

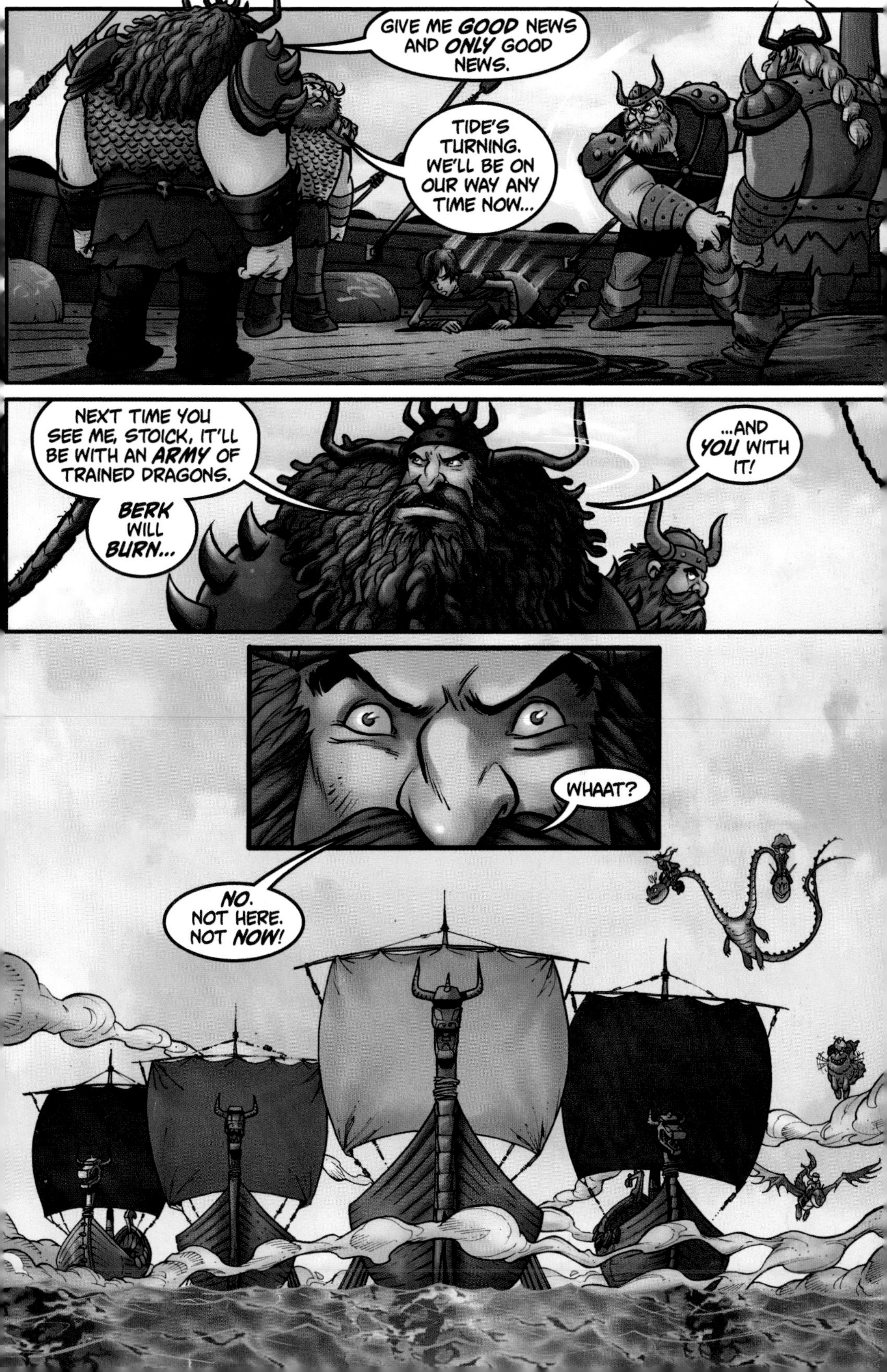
GIVE ME *GOOD* NEWS AND *ONLY* GOOD NEWS.
TIDE'S TURNING. WE'LL BE ON OUR WAY ANY TIME NOW...
NEXT TIME YOU SEE ME, STOICK, IT'LL BE WITH AN *ARMY* OF TRAINED DRAGONS.
BERK WILL *BURN*...
...AND *YOU* WITH IT!
WHAAT?
NO. NOT HERE. NOT *NOW!*

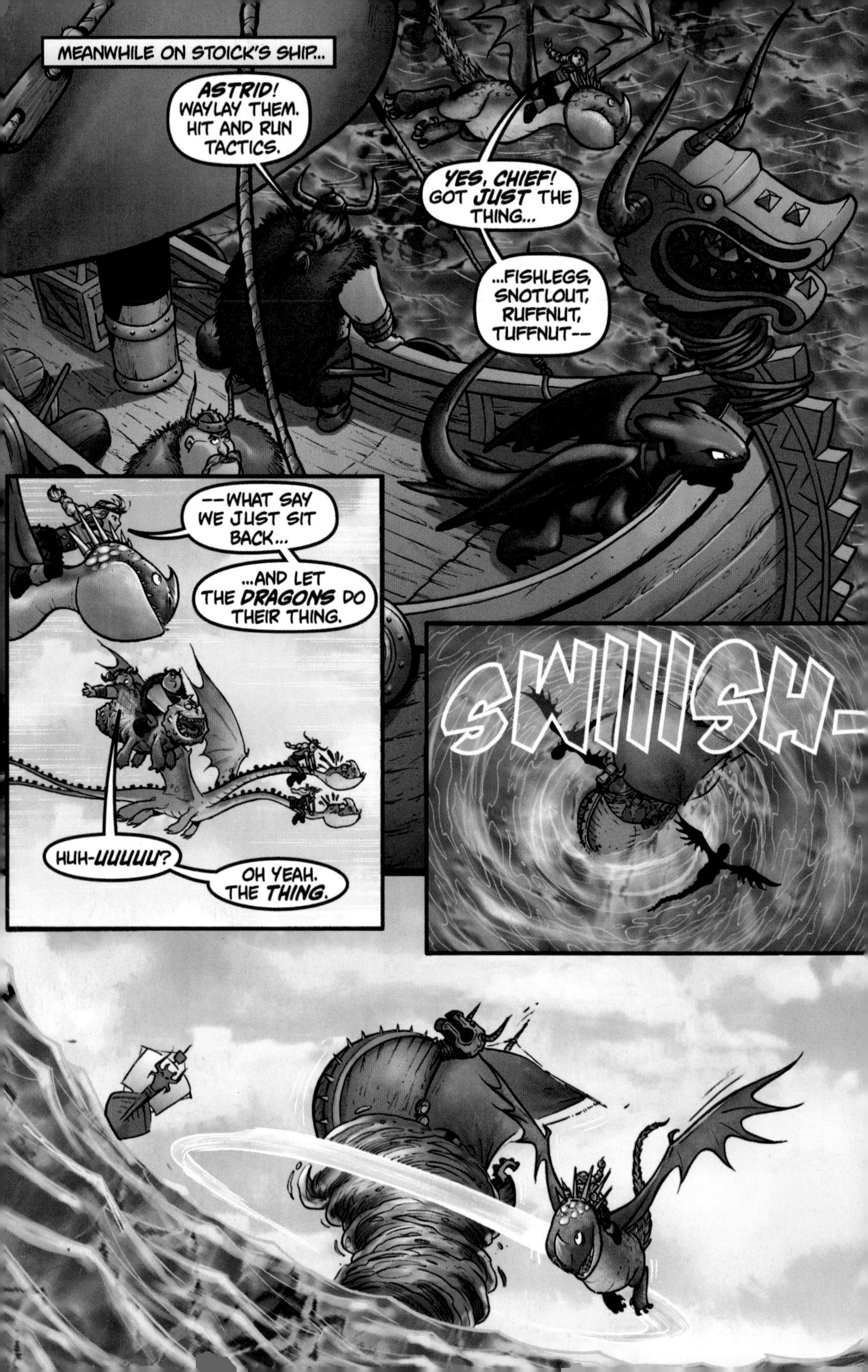
MEANWHILE ON STOICK'S SHIP...
ASTRID! WAYLAY THEM. HIT AND RUN TACTICS.
YES, CHIEF! GOT JUST THE THING...
...FISHLEGS, SNOTLOUT, RUFFNUT, TUFFNUT--
--WHAT SAY WE JUST SIT BACK...
...AND LET THE DRAGONS DO THEIR THING.
HUH-UUUUU?
OH YEAH. THE THING.
SWIIISH-

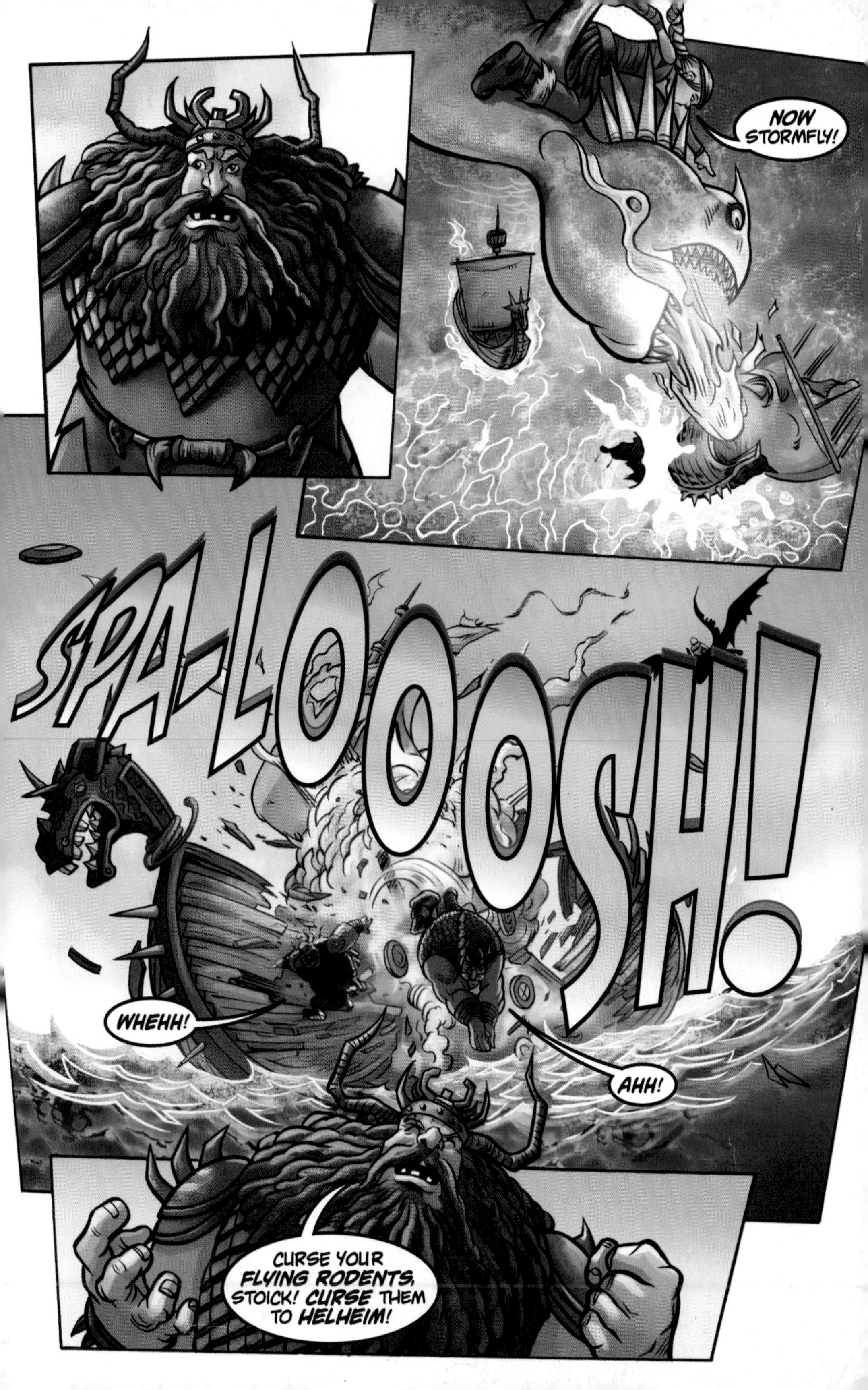
NOW STORMFLY!
SPA-LOOOSH!
WHEHH!
AHH!
CURSE YOUR FLYING RODENTS, STOICK! CURSE THEM TO HELHEIM!

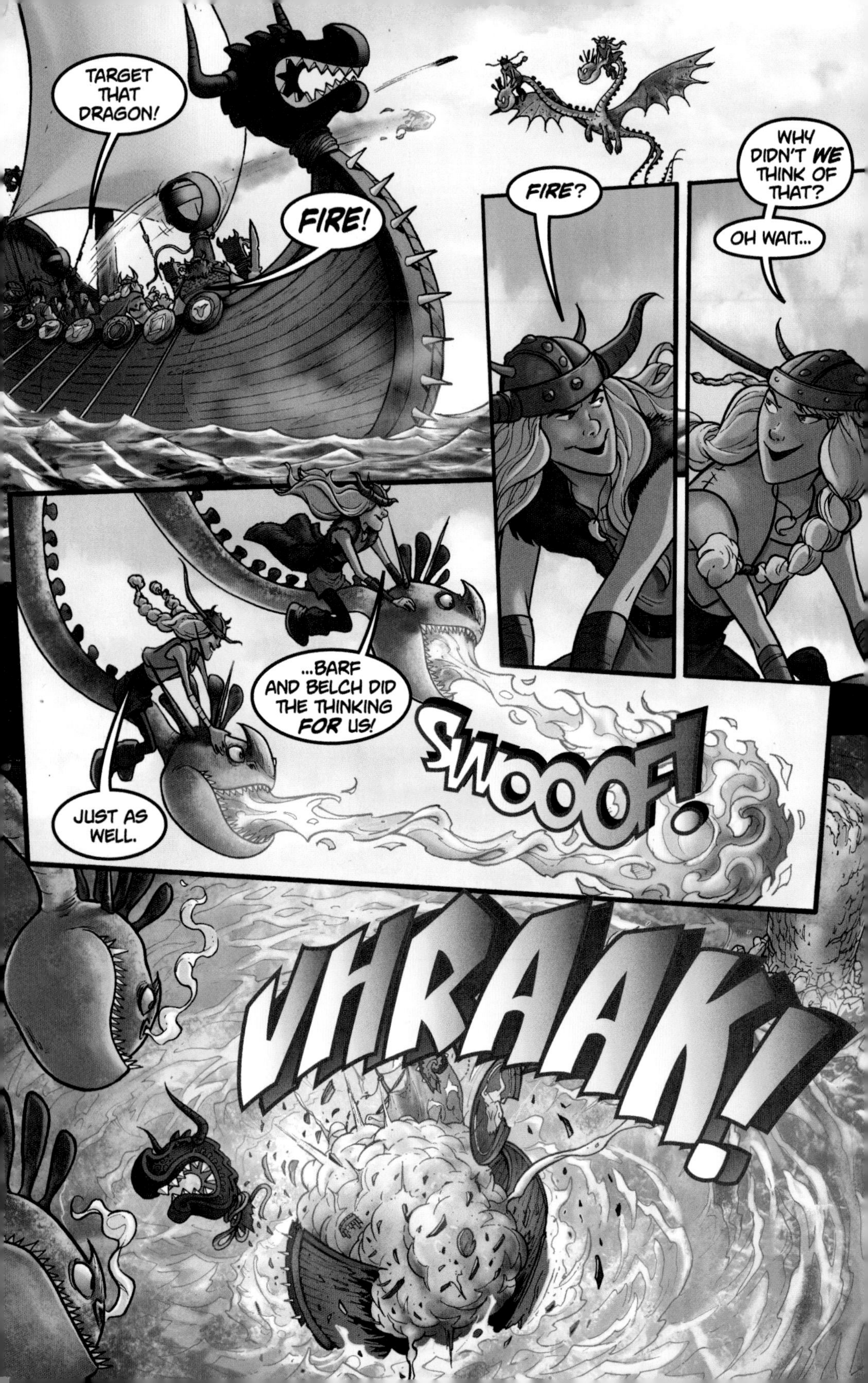
TARGET THAT DRAGON!
FIRE!
FIRE?
WHY DIDN'T WE THINK OF THAT?
OH WAIT...
...BARF AND BELCH DID THE THINKING FOR US!
JUST AS WELL.
SWOOOF!
JHRAAK!

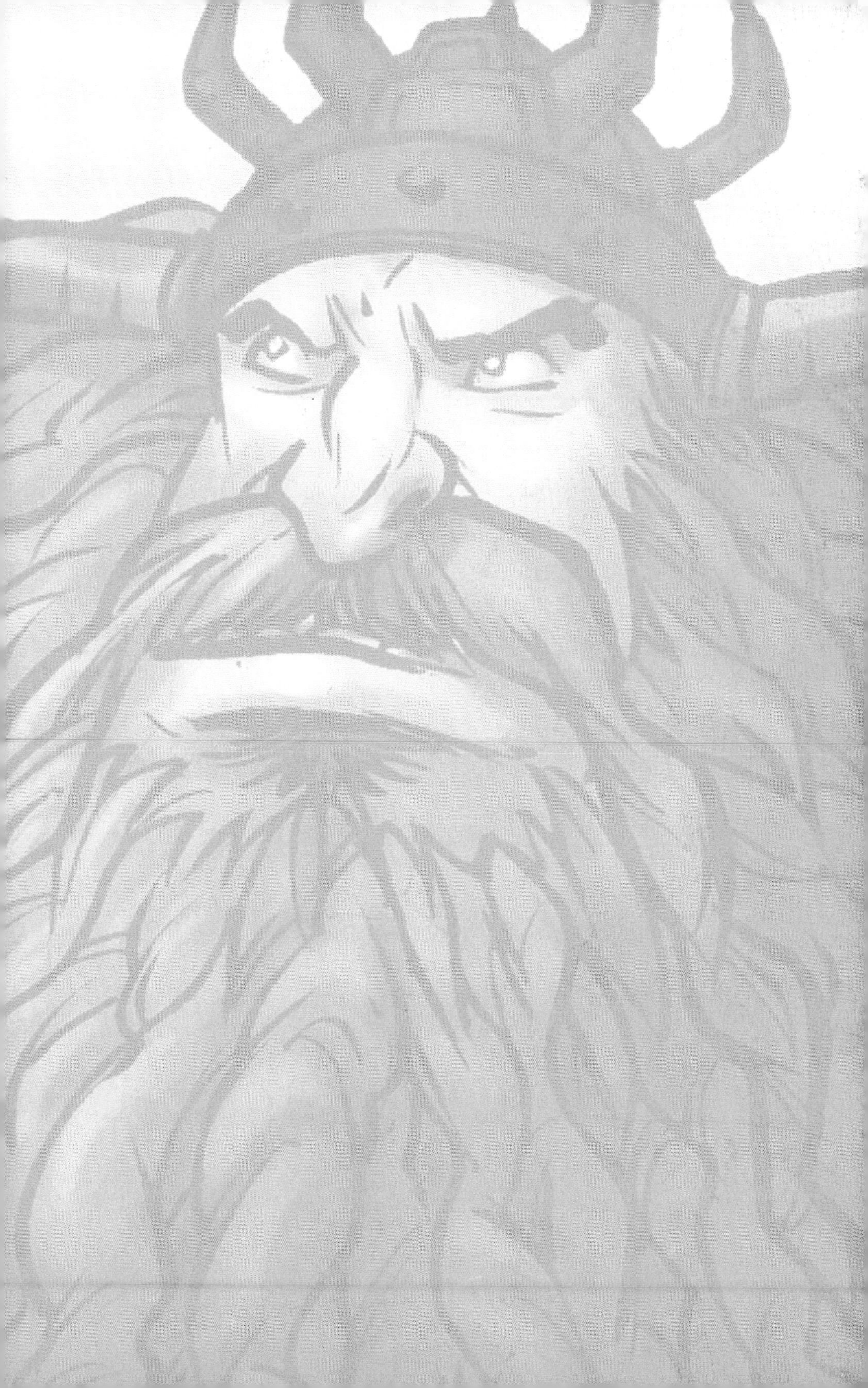

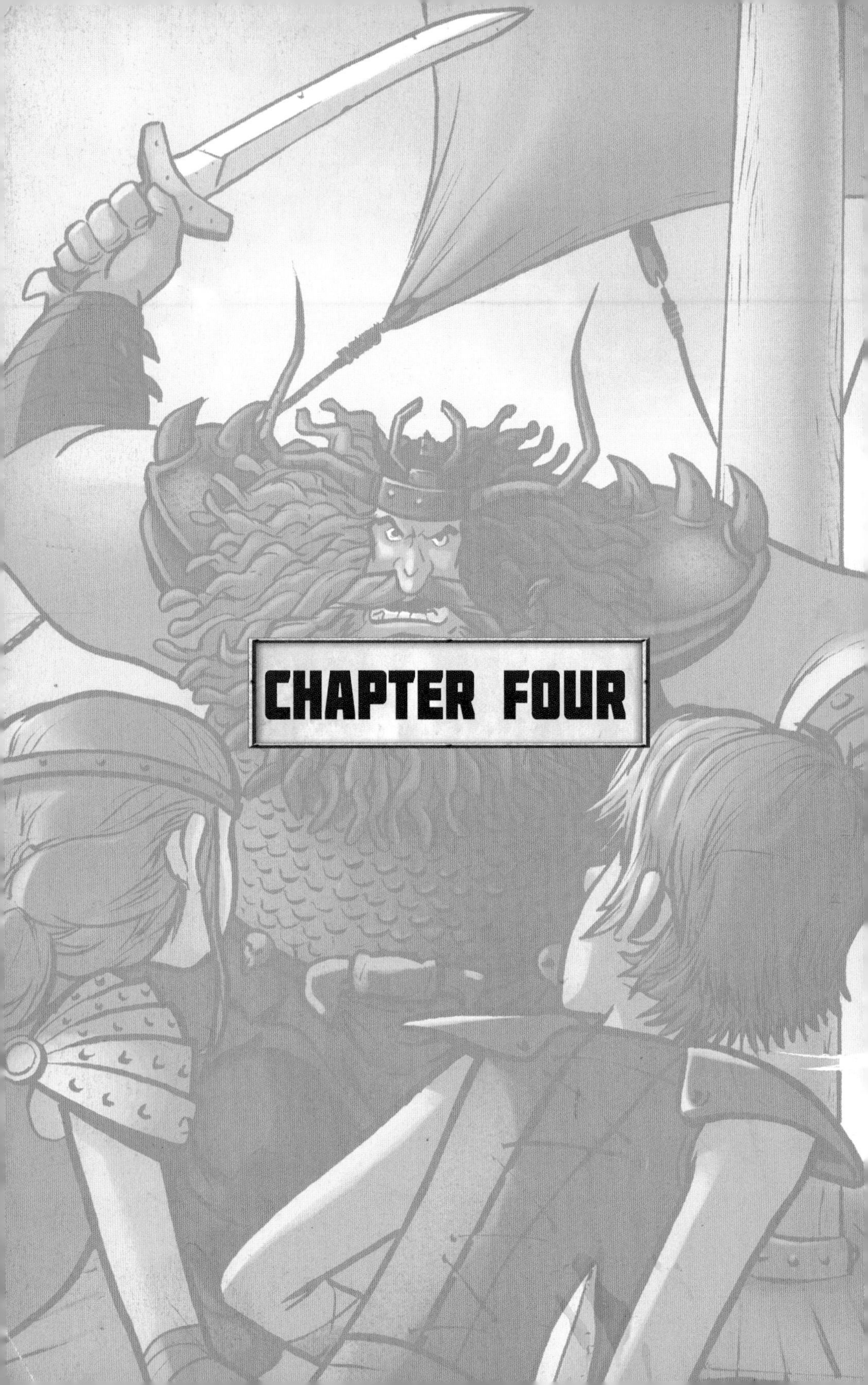

CHAPTER FOUR

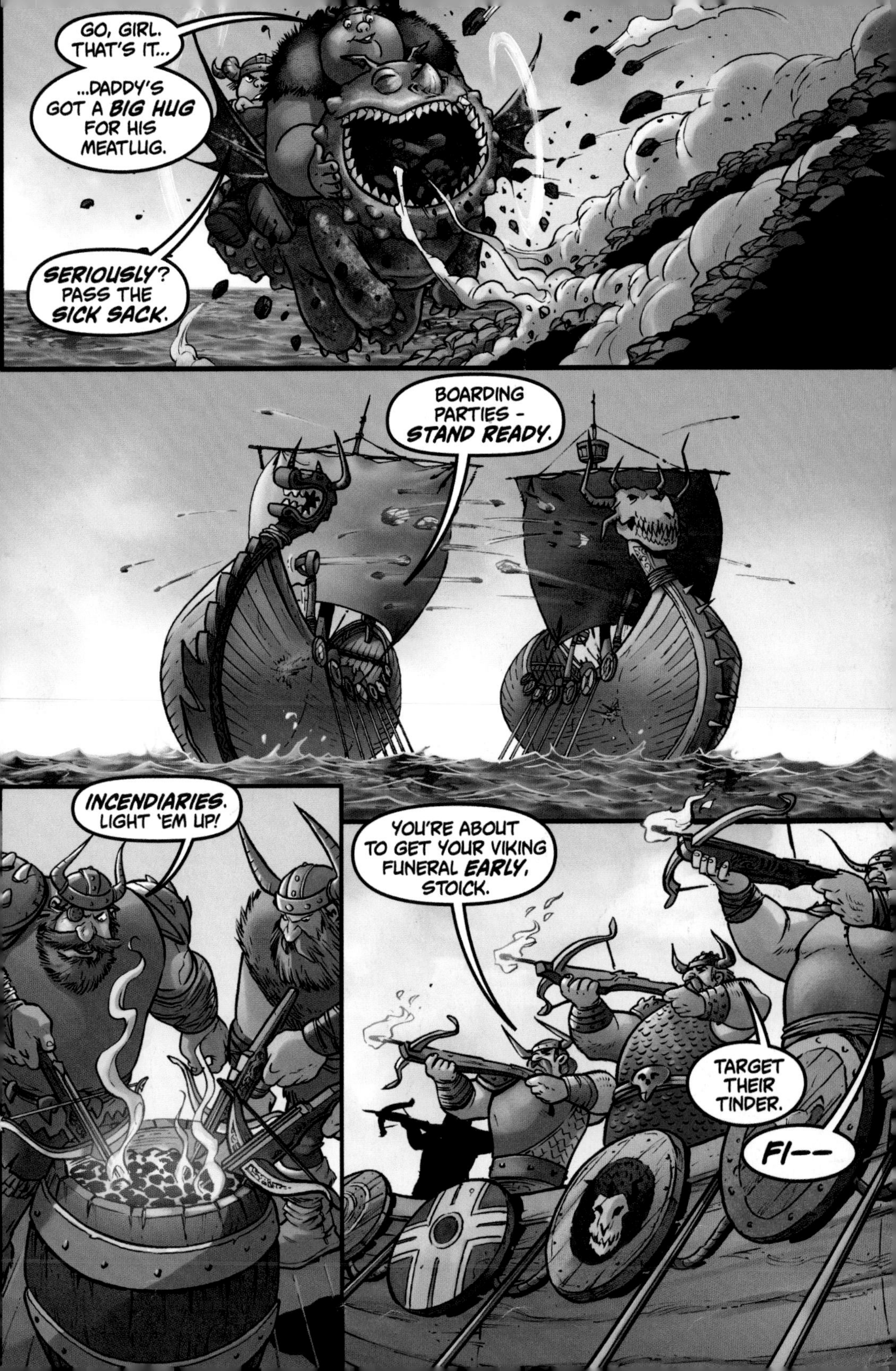
GO, GIRL. THAT'S IT...
...DADDY'S GOT A BIG HUG FOR HIS MEATLUG.
SERIOUSLY? PASS THE SICK SACK.
BOARDING PARTIES - STAND READY.
INCENDIARIES. LIGHT 'EM UP!
YOU'RE ABOUT TO GET YOUR VIKING FUNERAL EARLY, STOICK.
TARGET THEIR TINDER.
FI--

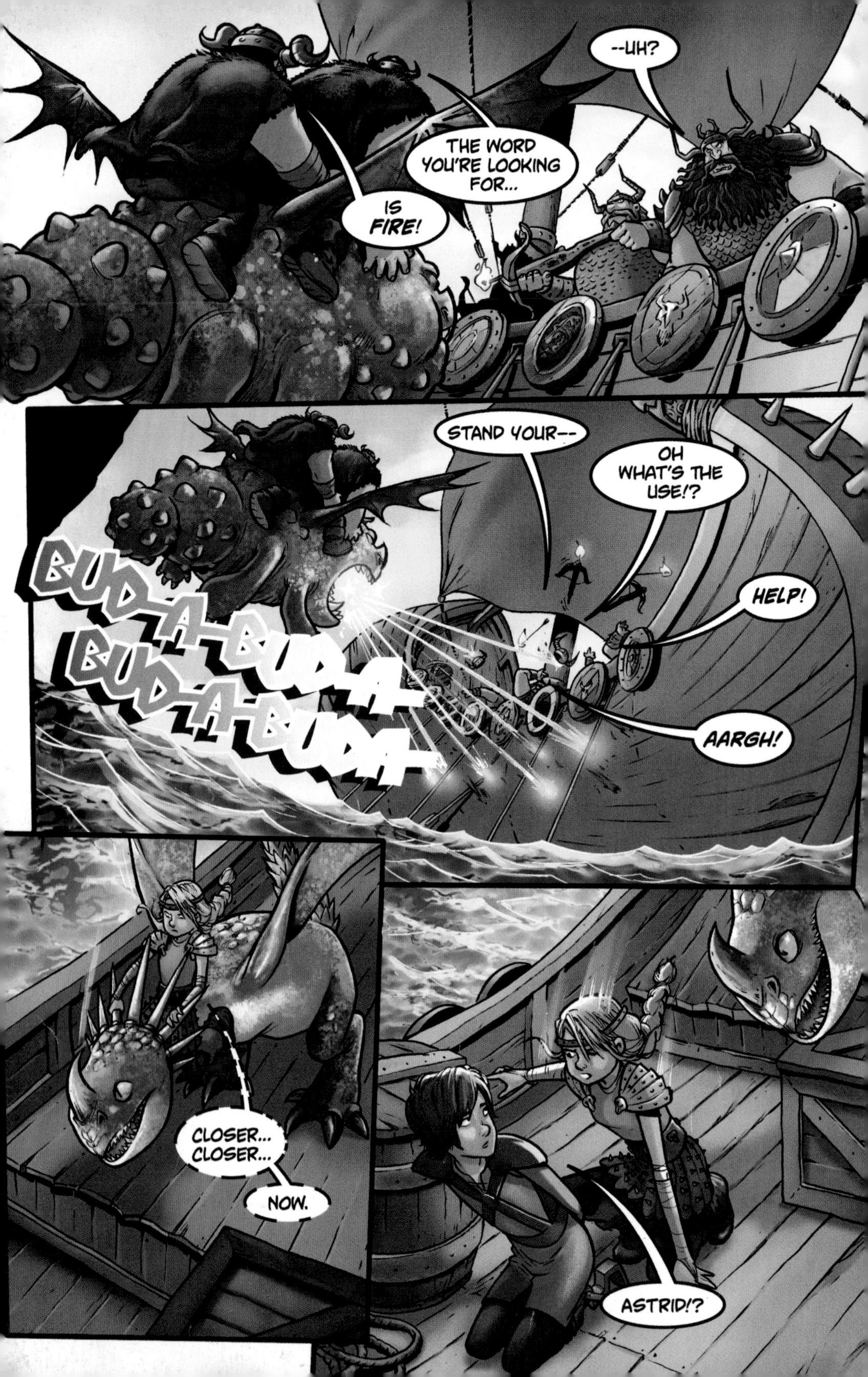

--UH?
THE WORD YOU'RE LOOKING FOR...
IS FIRE!
STAND YOUR--
OH WHAT'S THE USE!?
BUD-A-BUD-A BUD-A-BUDA
HELP!
AARGH!
CLOSER... CLOSER...
NOW.
ASTRID!?

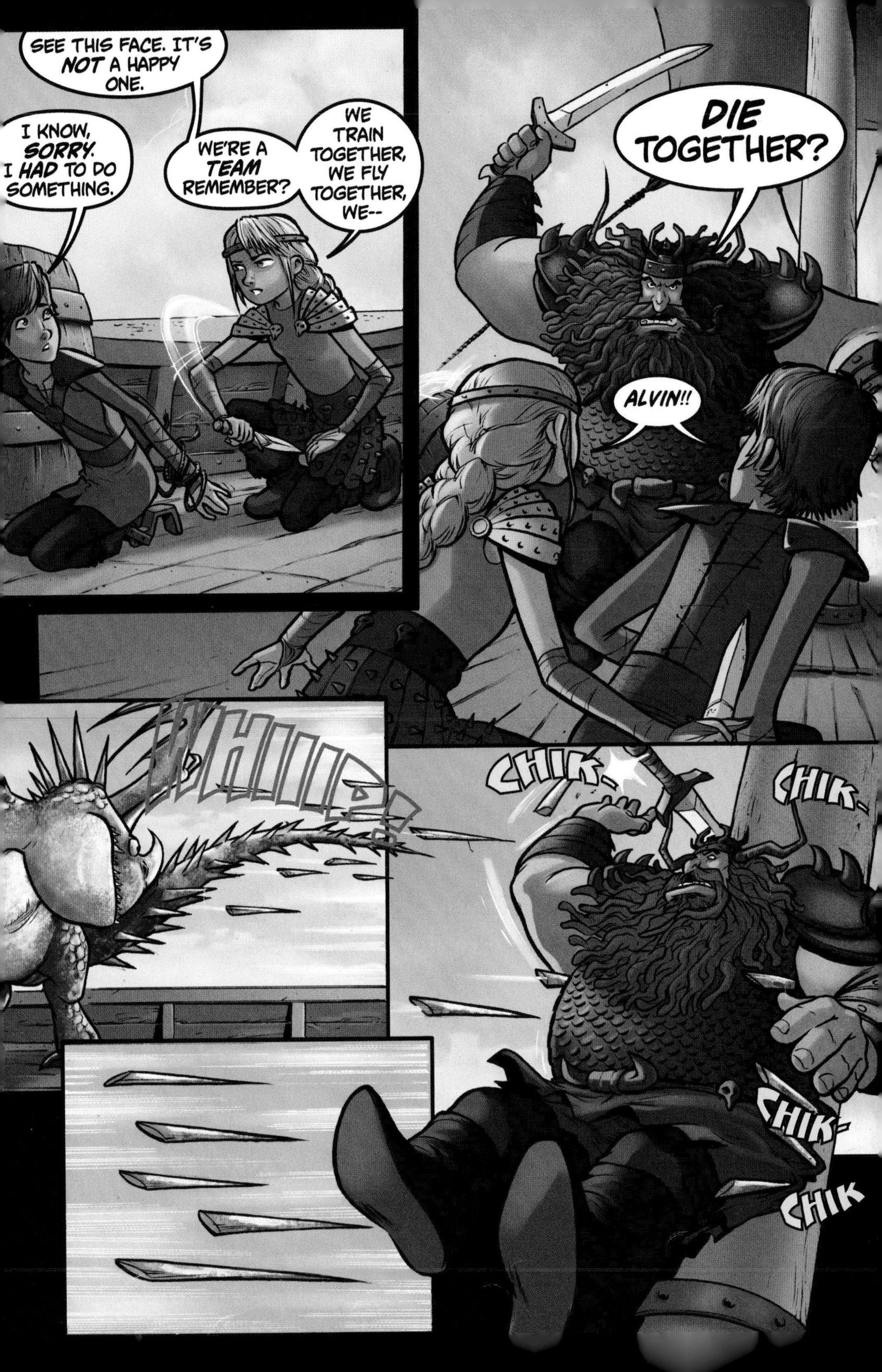
SEE THIS FACE. IT'S NOT A HAPPY ONE.
I KNOW, SORRY. I HAD TO DO SOMETHING.
WE'RE A TEAM REMEMBER?
WE TRAIN TOGETHER, WE FLY TOGETHER, WE--
DIE TOGETHER?
ALVIN!!
CHIK-
CHIK-
CHIK-
CHIK

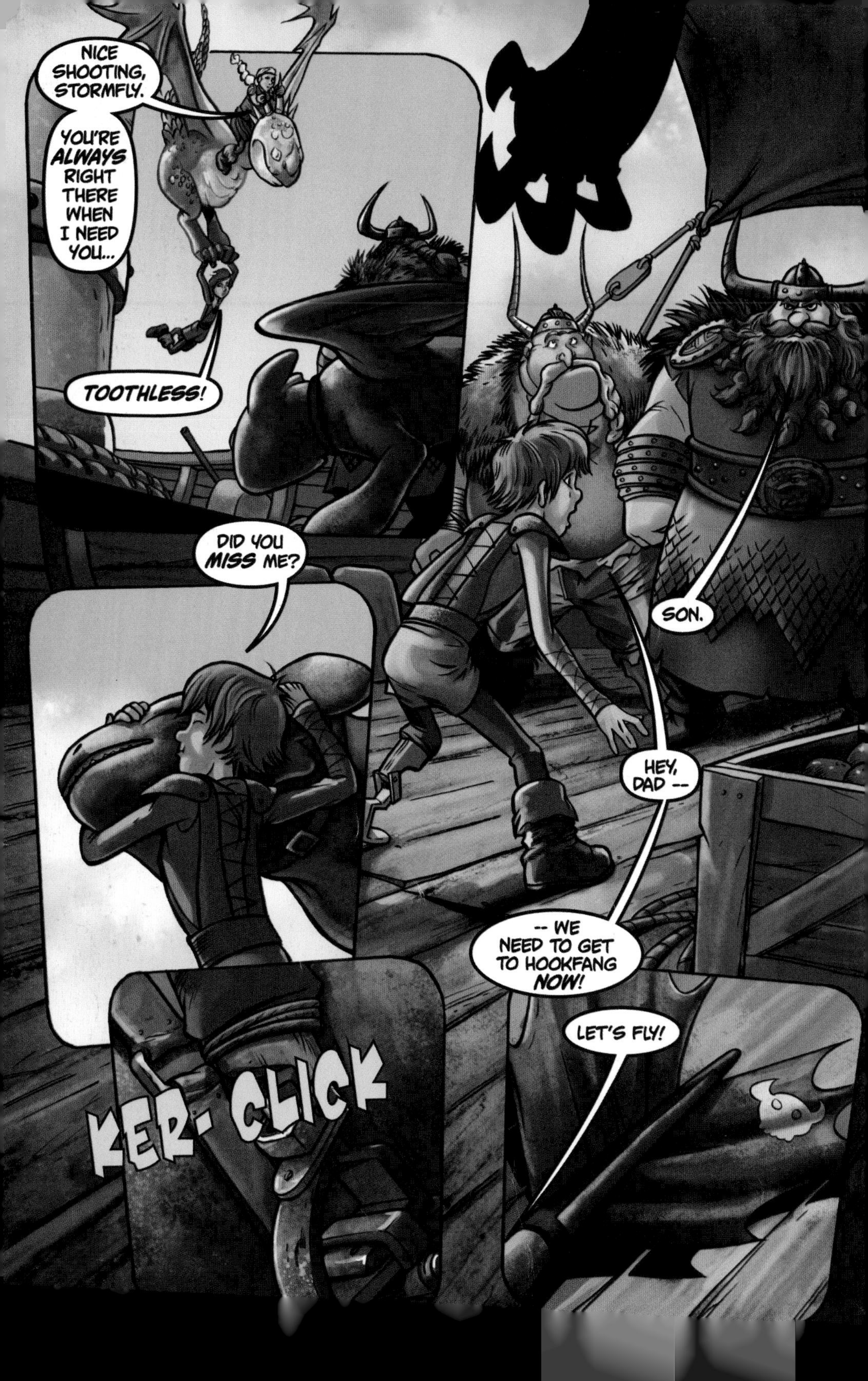
NICE SHOOTING, STORMFLY.
YOU'RE ALWAYS RIGHT THERE WHEN I NEED YOU...
TOOTHLESS!
DID YOU MISS ME?
SON.
HEY, DAD --
-- WE NEED TO GET TO HOOKFANG NOW!
KER-CLICK
LET'S FLY!

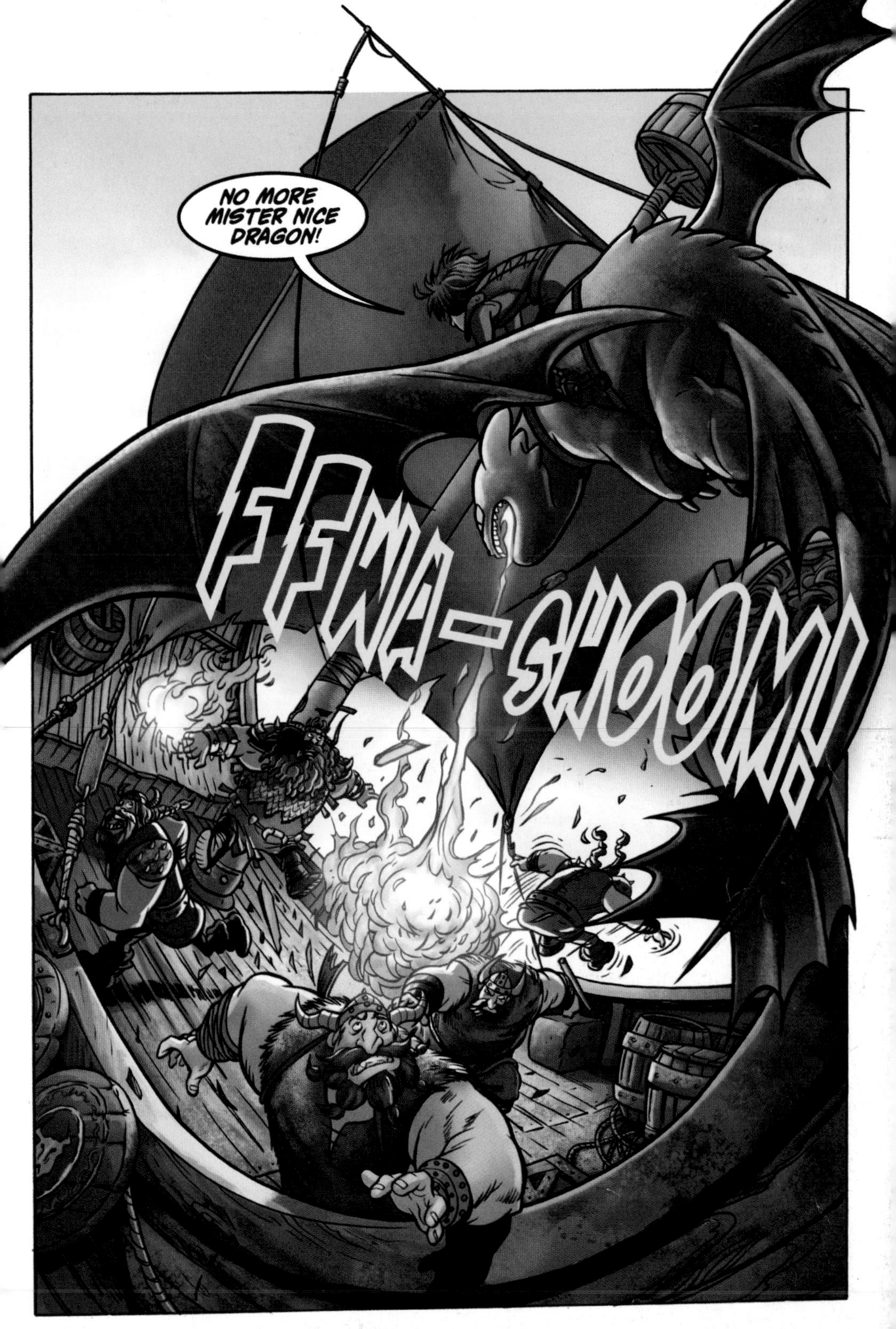
NO MORE MISTER NICE DRAGON!
FFWA-SHOOOM!

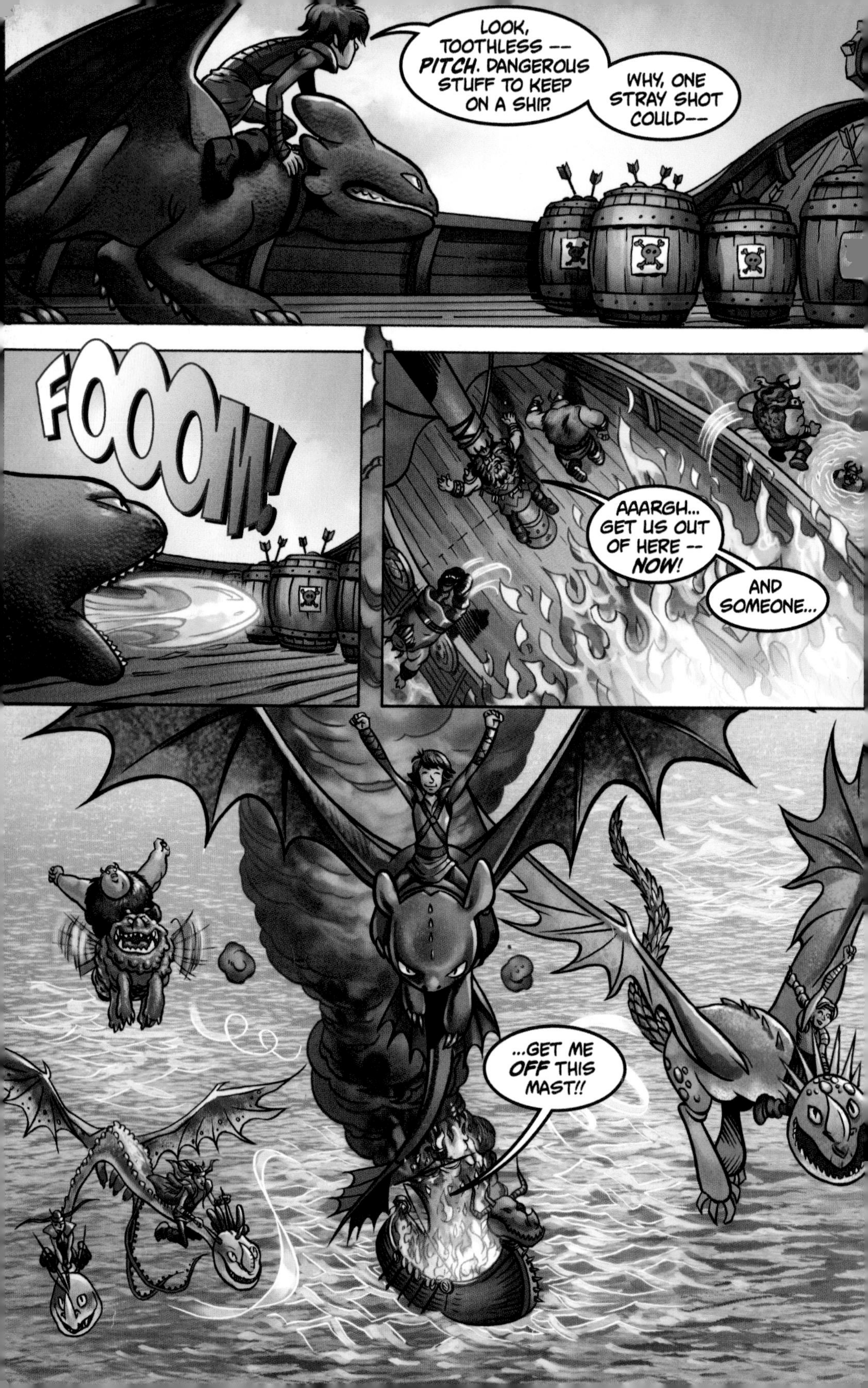
LOOK, TOOTHLESS -- PITCH. DANGEROUS STUFF TO KEEP ON A SHIP.
WHY, ONE STRAY SHOT COULD--
FOOOM!
AAARGH... GET US OUT OF HERE -- NOW!
AND SOMEONE...
...GET ME OFF THIS MAST!!

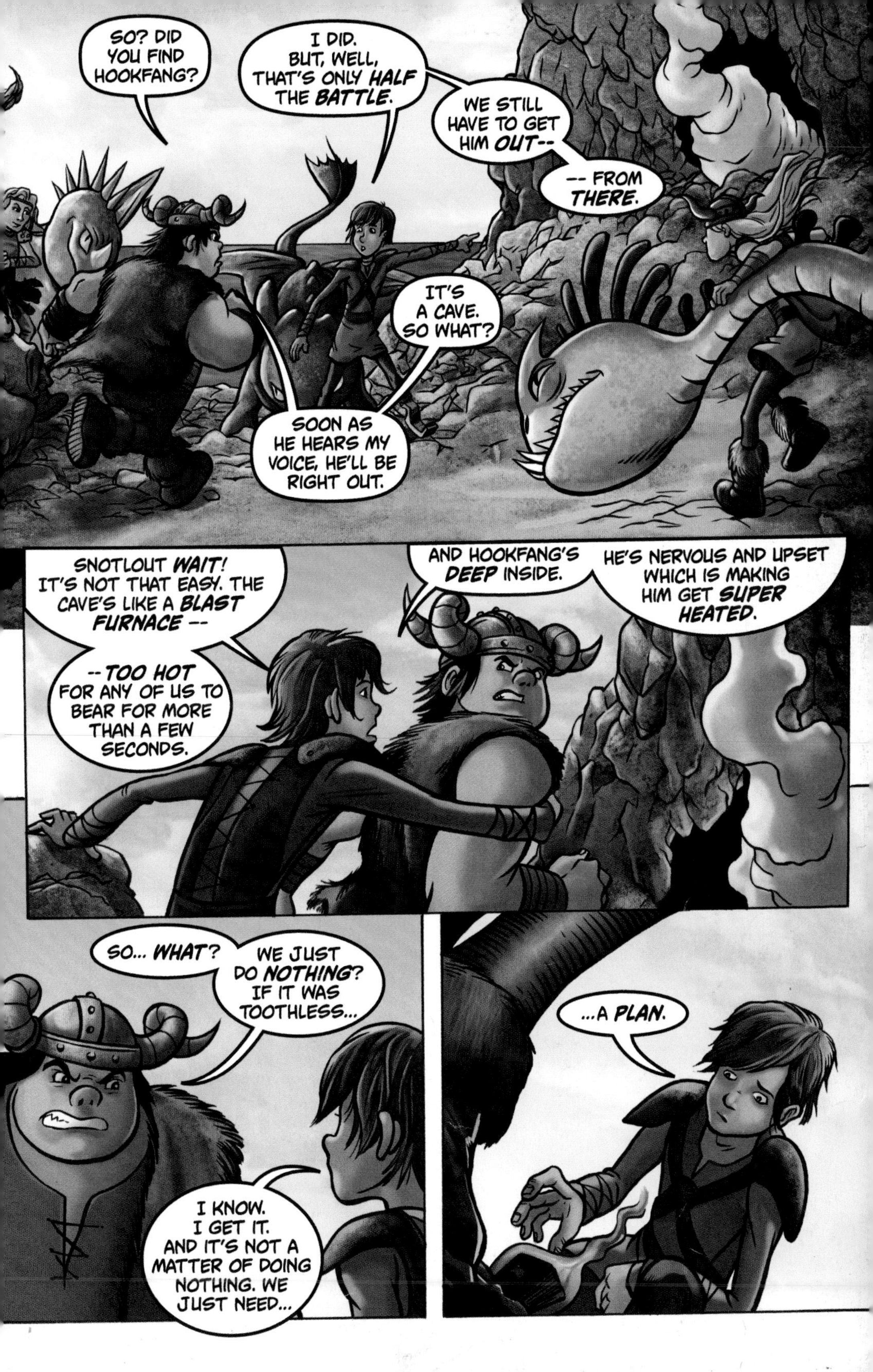
SO? DID YOU FIND HOOKFANG?
I DID. BUT, WELL, THAT'S ONLY HALF THE BATTLE.
WE STILL HAVE TO GET HIM OUT--
-- FROM THERE.
IT'S A CAVE. SO WHAT?
SOON AS HE HEARS MY VOICE, HE'LL BE RIGHT OUT.
SNOTLOUT WAIT! IT'S NOT THAT EASY. THE CAVE'S LIKE A BLAST FURNACE --
--TOO HOT FOR ANY OF US TO BEAR FOR MORE THAN A FEW SECONDS.
AND HOOKFANG'S DEEP INSIDE.
HE'S NERVOUS AND UPSET WHICH IS MAKING HIM GET SUPER HEATED.
SO... WHAT?
WE JUST DO NOTHING? IF IT WAS TOOTHLESS...
I KNOW. I GET IT. AND IT'S NOT A MATTER OF DOING NOTHING. WE JUST NEED...
...A PLAN.

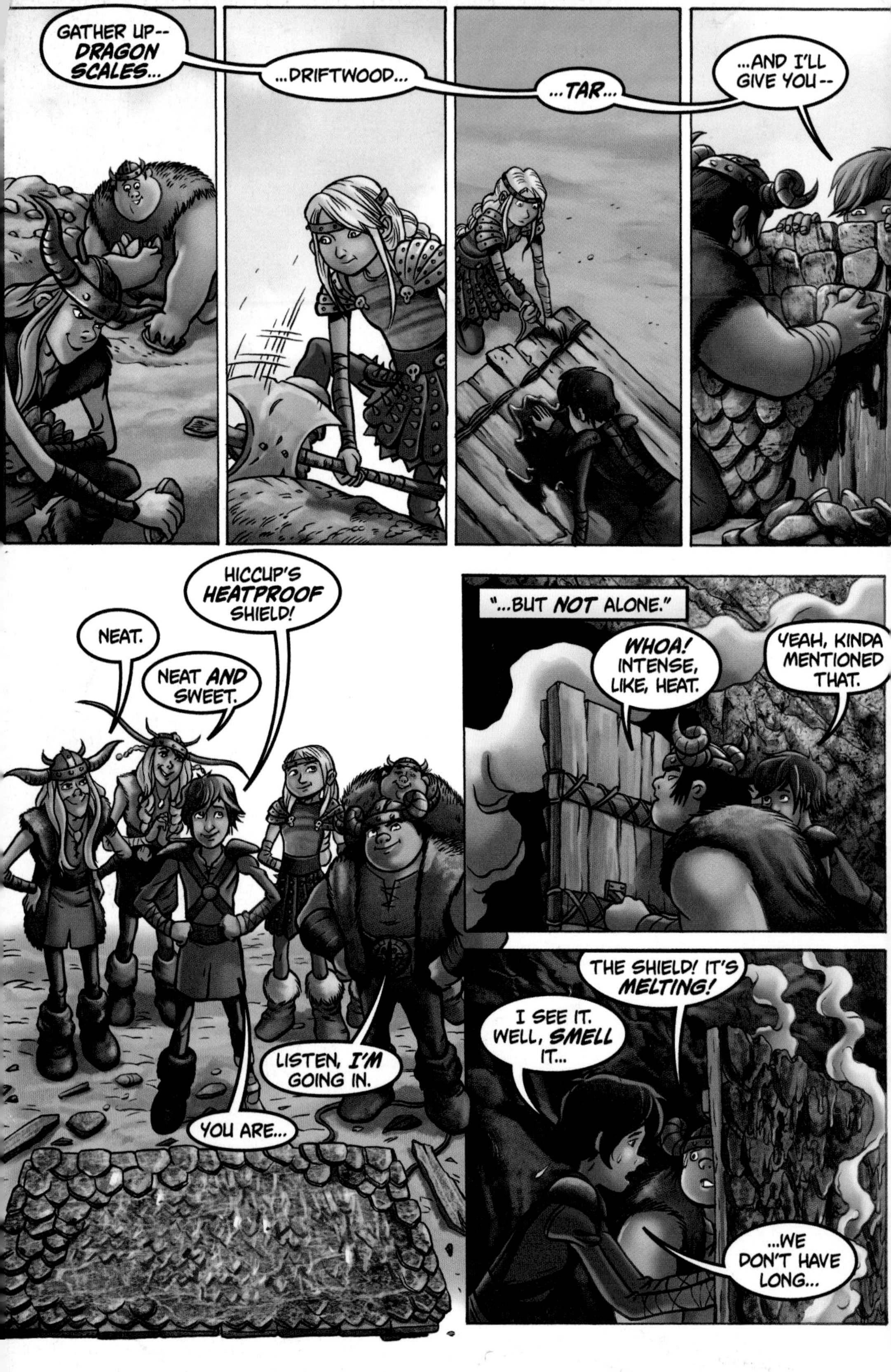
GATHER UP-- DRAGON SCALES...
...DRIFTWOOD...
...TAR...
...AND I'LL GIVE YOU--
HICCUP'S HEATPROOF SHIELD!
NEAT.
NEAT AND SWEET.
LISTEN, I'M GOING IN.
YOU ARE...
"...BUT NOT ALONE."
WHOA! INTENSE, LIKE, HEAT.
YEAH, KINDA MENTIONED THAT.
THE SHIELD! IT'S MELTING!
I SEE IT. WELL, SMELL IT...
...WE DON'T HAVE LONG...

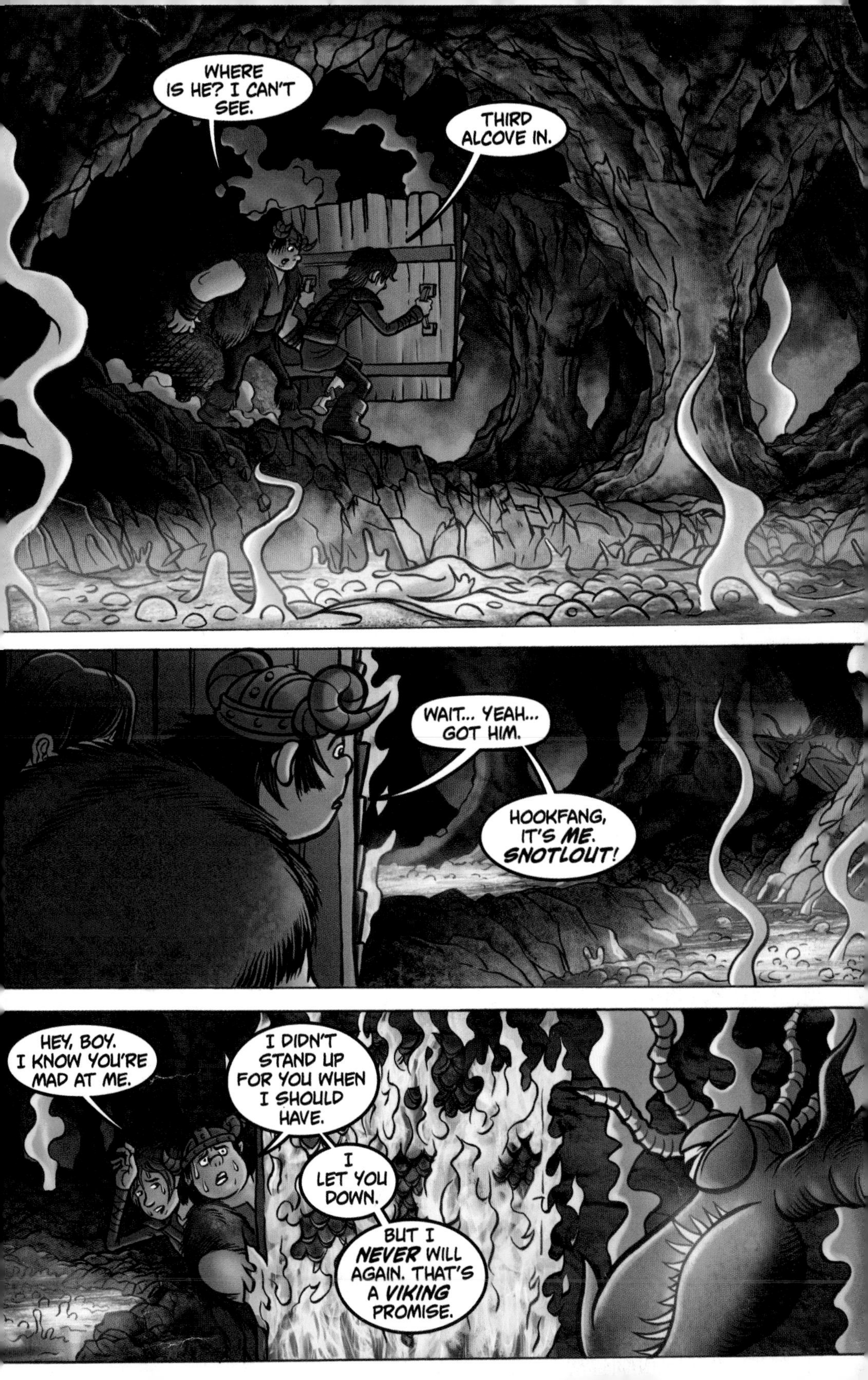
WHERE IS HE? I CAN'T SEE.
THIRD ALCOVE IN.
WAIT... YEAH... GOT HIM.
HOOKFANG, IT'S *ME*. *SNOTLOUT*!
HEY, BOY. I KNOW YOU'RE MAD AT ME.
I DIDN'T STAND UP FOR YOU WHEN I SHOULD HAVE.
I LET YOU DOWN.
BUT I *NEVER* WILL AGAIN. THAT'S A *VIKING* PROMISE.

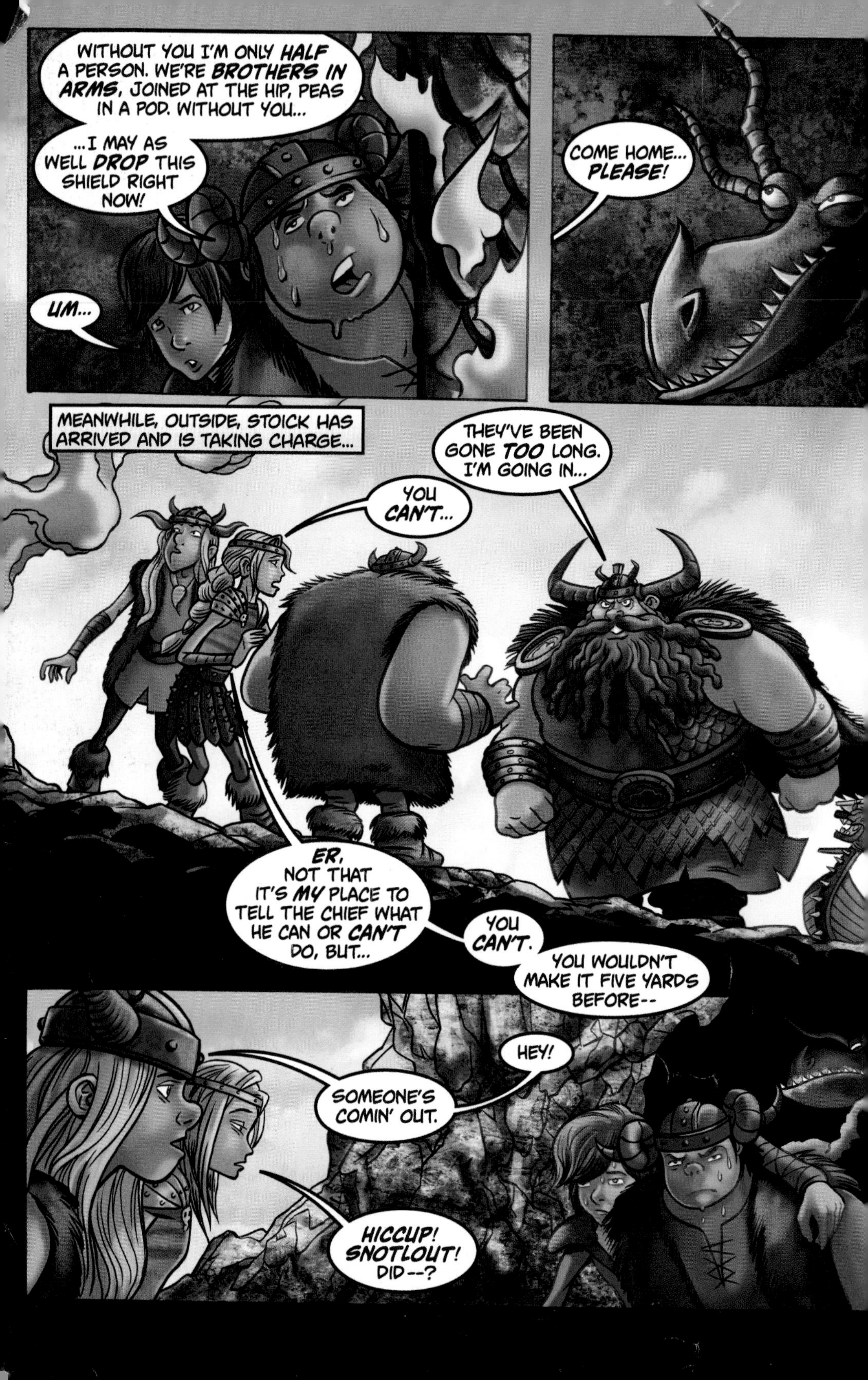
WITHOUT YOU I'M ONLY HALF A PERSON. WE'RE BROTHERS IN ARMS, JOINED AT THE HIP, PEAS IN A POD. WITHOUT YOU...
...I MAY AS WELL DROP THIS SHIELD RIGHT NOW!
UM...
COME HOME... PLEASE!
MEANWHILE, OUTSIDE, STOICK HAS ARRIVED AND IS TAKING CHARGE...
THEY'VE BEEN GONE TOO LONG. I'M GOING IN...
YOU CAN'T...
ER, NOT THAT IT'S MY PLACE TO TELL THE CHIEF WHAT HE CAN OR CAN'T DO, BUT...
YOU CAN'T.
YOU WOULDN'T MAKE IT FIVE YARDS BEFORE--
HEY!
SOMEONE'S COMIN' OUT.
HICCUP! SNOTLOUT! DID--?

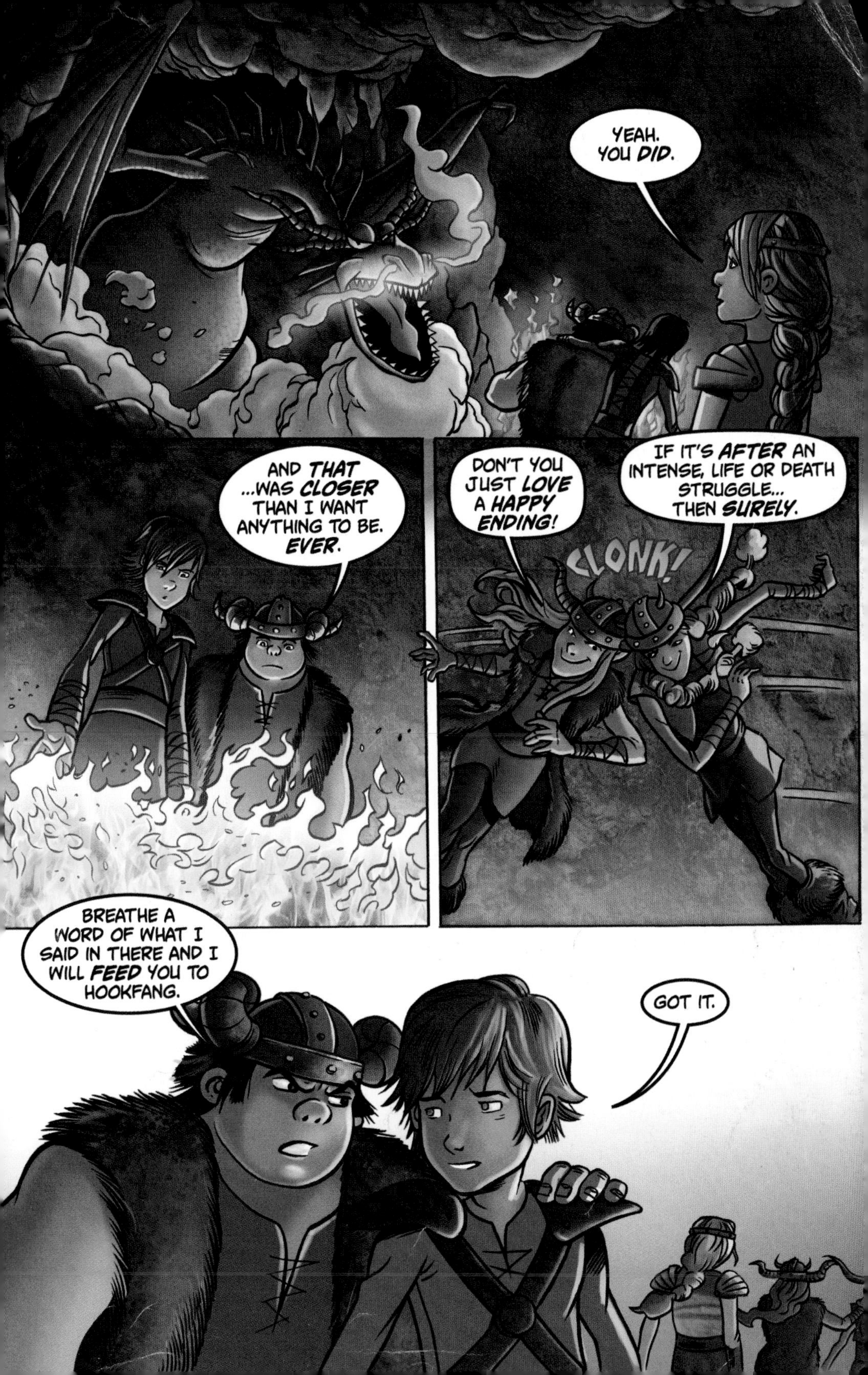
YEAH. YOU DID.
AND THAT ...WAS CLOSER THAN I WANT ANYTHING TO BE. EVER.
DON'T YOU JUST LOVE A HAPPY ENDING!
IF IT'S AFTER AN INTENSE, LIFE OR DEATH STRUGGLE... THEN SURELY.
CLONK!
BREATHE A WORD OF WHAT I SAID IN THERE AND I WILL FEED YOU TO HOOKFANG.
GOT IT.

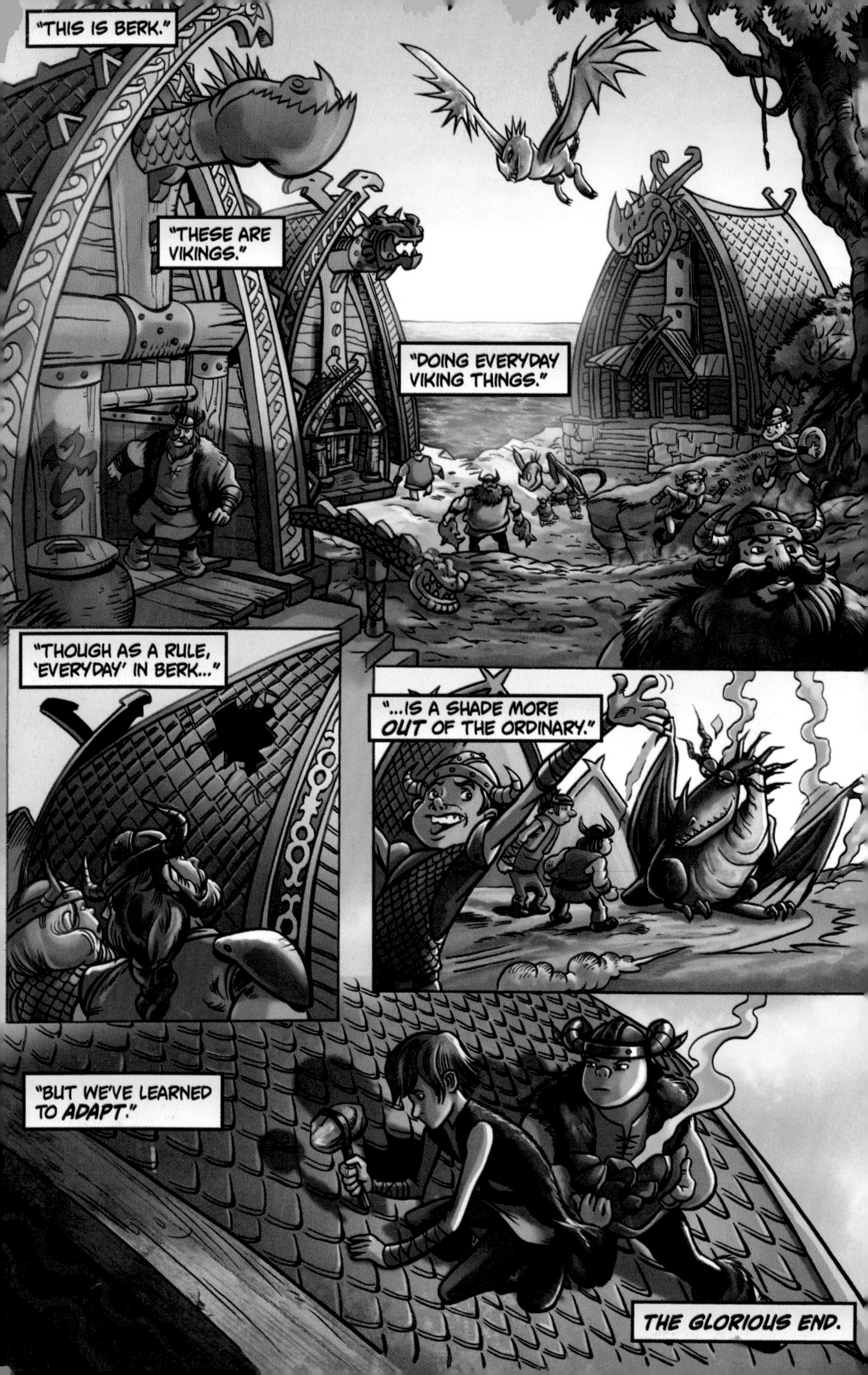
"THIS IS BERK."
"THESE ARE VIKINGS."
"DOING EVERYDAY VIKING THINGS."
"THOUGH AS A RULE, 'EVERYDAY' IN BERK..."
"...IS A SHADE MORE OUT OF THE ORDINARY."
"BUT WE'VE LEARNED TO ADAPT."
THE GLORIOUS END.

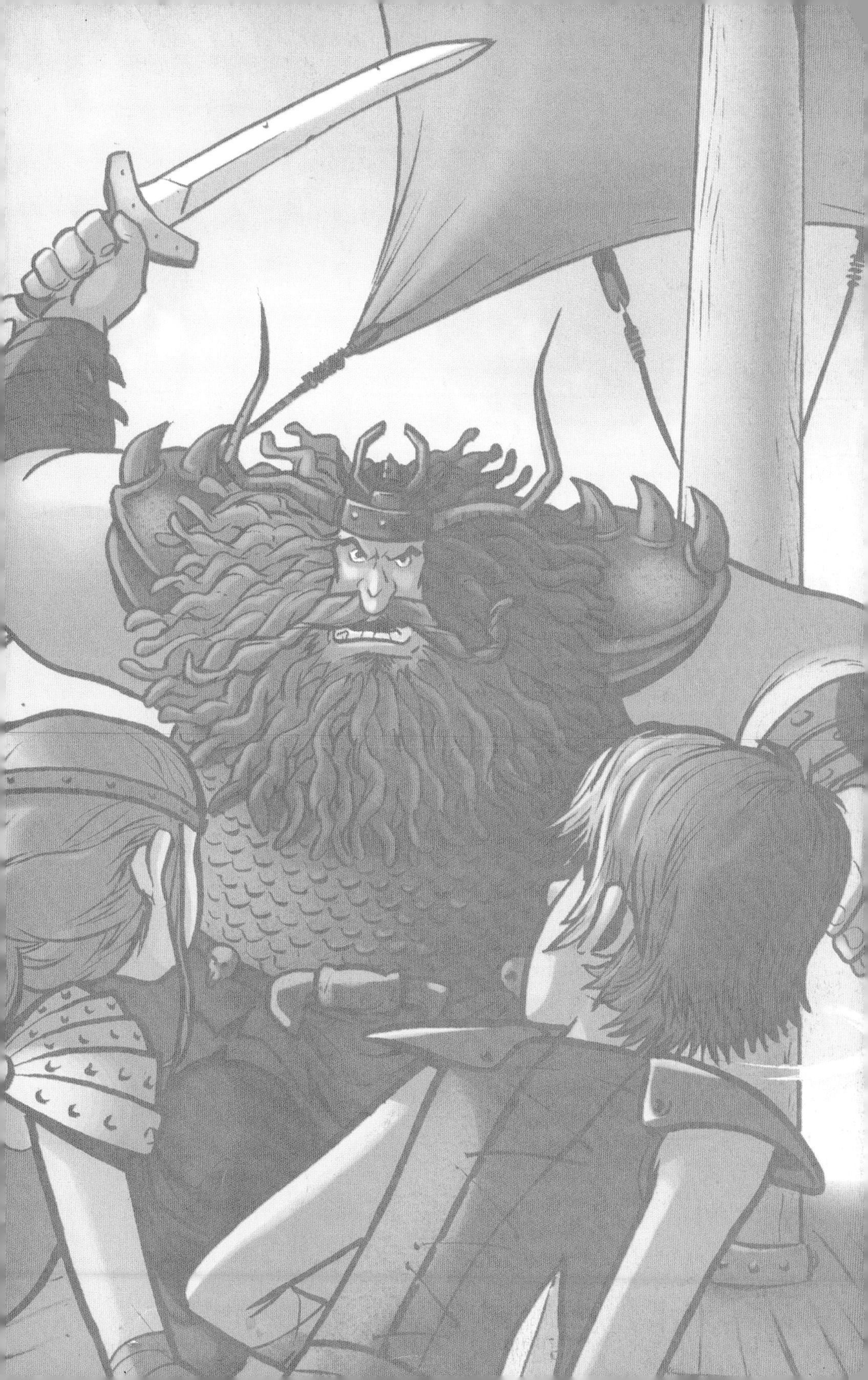

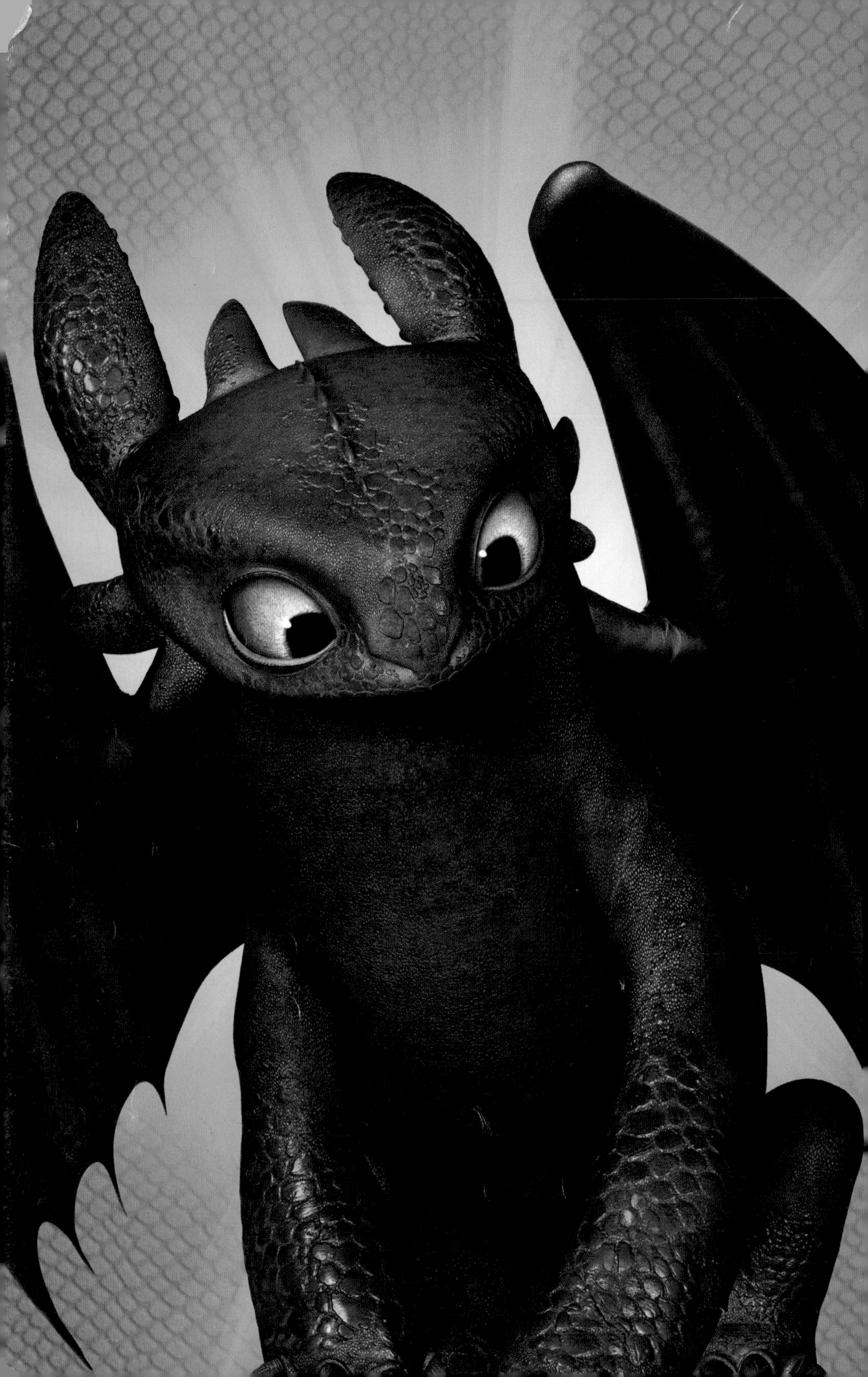

ALSO AVAILABLE SOON!

VOLUME TWO

Hiccup is left in charge of Berk! Sounds cool? Yep — until Alvin the Treacherous decides to attack the town...

Meanwhile, in the scary Veil of Mists, Stoick and Co are being stalked by something huge and deadly...!

DreamWorks
DRAGONS
RIDERS OF BERK

VOLUME 2

OUT AUGUST 26TH!

PLUS: COMING SOON!

VOLUME THREE
ON SALE NOVEMBER 18th

DreamWorks
DRAGONS
RIDERS OF BERK

VOLUME 3

ALSO UPCOMING:

VOLUME FOUR
(FEBRUARY 2015)
VOLUME FIVE
(MAY 2015)
VOLUME SIX
(AUGUST 2015)